"Nibelung," Emn
whisper that held more power than the ....

The slivers of starlight that had managed to force their way into the building now began to change direction. Several different beams met within the center of Emmett's circle. At the point where each beam of light departed its natural course, they had transformed into tight rays of brilliant shifting colors. Tiny, terrifying rainbows in the darkness, they illuminated the icy void beneath the circle and drew out the thing that Emmett had summoned.

And so Nibelung rose from the circle, pulled up by prismatic bonds. Its body was humanoid, enormous but stout. Its ten-foot height was matched by the width of its shoulders. The creature's nightmare features and frostbitten skin were only partially illuminated by the shifting axis of light. Still Emmett knew it was the creature from his dream—the dwarf who had beckoned him greedily while he thrashed in the river of slush. The light reflected off of the riches worked into the dwarf's beard and the gaudy rings that bit into its meaty, calloused fingers.

Incomprehensible words, the sounds of breaking ice and something being dragged through gravel, erupted from the lips of the thing that Emmett knew as Nibelung. Sane words—words in Emmett's own tongue of Americanized English—echoed through the circle, following the dwarf's guttural barks like some sort of audial Rosetta Stone.

"He who summons Nibelung the betrayer best do so with good reason." The speech had a metallic quality to it, as if the metal shavings that made up the circle had affected the tone.

More barking leapt from the dwarf's mouth—cracking ice and breaking glass and gravel crunching under foot. The alien words were followed immediately by the metallic voice of the circle.

"It was I who first betrayed this world for the lords of Utgard. For that treachery I have eternity at my fingertips and riches more vast than all of the gold created from every star that has ever died."

The barking paused first, then the echoed speech.

After the space of ten seconds the dwarf croaked his inarticulate voice once more, and the surrounding voice followed suit.

"What could one such as you possibly offer one such as me?"

THE DEVOURED
CURTIS M. LAWSON

WYRD
Horror

DEDICATION

The Devoured is dedicated to Gary and Tristan,
the man who helped make me what I am,
and the boy who made me better than I am.

*Special thanks to Christine for putting up with my neglect
and fits of indecision while writing this, to Josh and Jack for beta-
reading, and to Monique and Brad for their help with the first
edition.*

***

A WYRD HORROR BOOK

THE DEVOURED
First edition published by Winlock Press, 2015
Second edition published by Wyrd Horror, 2017

ISBN: 9781520629209

© 2015, 2017 by Curtis M. Lawson
All Rights Reserved

Edited by Monique Happy Editorial Services
Cover art by Angel Aviles

CHAPTER ONE

The old man could evoke no mystic powers, nor weave hexes of his own. Months spent scouring the most forsaken regions of the southwest had armed him with enough knowledge to disrupt the magic of others, though. With strong hands the color and texture of rawhide, the old man popped the iron cap off of one of his rounds. In a careful, deliberate manner, he poured black powder from the bullet, tracing a portion of the blood-etched circle that guarded the shack.

He pocketed the empty round for reuse later and withdrew a box of matches. There was a fair bit of wind that day, cold fronts from the east dancing violently with warm, native air, so the old man knelt down close to the powder before striking his match. With a hiss and a puff of smoke, the gunpowder dispelled the ward so that he could safely cross.

The old man stepped over the scorched blood and moved toward the decrepit, one room shack. Early morning sunlight streamed through the canopy of leaves above, hitting the broken facade like a sepia tone kaleidoscope.

The door was uneven in the frame and didn't close correctly. A nauseating stench, that of gangrenous flesh, wafted out from the shack, mixed with the pleasant smells of spices and broth. Like farmers and apothecaries, witches tended to be fine cooks.

The porch protested with a loud creak as the old man stepped up to the entrance. An even louder screech came from the rusted hinges of the shabby door. The witch slept soundly through the warnings that its abode issued, much to the old man's relief.

The old man placed his pack on the floor and surveyed the witch's home. A large, black pot was propped up over a makeshift fireplace, the remnants of a hearty rabbit stew from the night before still lining it. Bones of rabbits and squirrels lay in one corner, mixed with poorly skinned hides waiting for repurpose. An old board propped up on two wooden crates held leaded bottles and burlap pouches full of oils and spices. Rooted deep within the dirt floor, right in the center of the room, was a massive tree stump, a yard and a third across. It looked to serve as dinner table, work desk, and altar. The old man guessed that the stump had been key in deciding where to build the shack.

The witch itself lay deeply asleep on a small cot with its matted, white hair covering much of its face. The cot was the kind used for battlefield surgery, and it bore the stains of many a soldier's blood. The pillow that lay under the witch's head had at one time been a fine, frilly piece with golden tassels and embroidery. It was the kind of thing the old man had seen in the brothels of his youth. Now the pillow was stained and frayed. Its once deep burgundy tone had bleached over time into a dull, reddish gray. A reflection of the witch's own heart, perhaps.

The old man unsheathed the sword that was strapped to his back. The blade was a Confederate artillery sword, the last-ditch weapon of gunners who fought for the stars and bars. Modeled after the Roman gladius, it was a hefty weapon, thick in the middle. A design that had proven itself for millennia. Some didn't like its weight. The old man, however, was accustomed to heavy burdens, and it felt comfortable in his hands.

He positioned the sword's tip above the witch's belly. Taking a deep breath, he looked down upon the mangy, gangrenous wretch with its sunken eyes and matted hair. Its chapped lips parted, revealing its white tongue and rotted teeth. As he had done with every tainted thing that he had killed over the past months, the old man took a moment to see the woman beneath.

It was important to the old man that he recognize that every witch had once been something more than a vessel of chaos. They had been soldiers and farmers, mothers and fathers. At one point in time, each was a child whose smile meant the world to someone. Or perhaps some were the unwanted offspring of degenerates, making them easy pickings for the Devourers. Whatever their history, there was something human in there. Something more divine than any god or devil. For every evil thing he had crushed, the old man knew that he had also murdered the human left inside. He never wanted that to become easy.

With strong arms and steady hands, the old man drove the blade through the witch's belly and into the cot. He was careful to avoid any vital organs. It was important that the creature face a slow and painful death. The old man needed time to negotiate, and he knew pain to be a powerful tonic for loosening lips. The foul stench of infection escaped the witch's belly wound, just as a discordant howl of pain leapt forth from its chapped lips. Black ichor bubbled out around the blade, popping and splashing the old man's cracked hands. The touch of the blood felt like hot ash on his skin. The thing was sick and by all rights should have been already dead. This wasn't the first time the old man had seen death staved off by dark magics.

The dark eyelids of the diseased, backwoods sorceress shot open. The yellow orbs in its eye sockets were riddled with crisscrossing veins—tiny red tributaries leading toward the black oceans of its pupils. There was a deep and complex madness in the witch's gaze, though it did not mask the fear or pain that it felt.

"Shallow breaths might be best," the old man stated in a calm and even manner. "Breathe too heavy or get all cantankerous and this here blade might serrate more o' them rotten, squishy bits inside you."

A wicked sneer crossed the witch's mouth, revealing black and yellow teeth in various states of decay. Pain and fear were displaced with an unholy rage—an urge to destroy that outweighed self-preservation. With its left hand, the thing that had once been a woman bent its middle finger, so that its filthy tip touched the first bloated and arthritic knuckle on its index finger.

Before any ancient word could lend power to the witch's gesture, the old man's hand struck out with a speed that seemed at odds with his age. Hands like iron crushed the feeble digits of the dying sorceress. Bones cracked beneath diseased skin, leaving the witch's hand like a pouch of crushed stone. The pain caused the witch to involuntarily screech and squirm, which in turn caused the confederate gladius to tear at its insides. Before the creature could recover from the agony of its broken fingers, the old man grabbed its other hand. With one swift motion he bent the witch's fingers back until they snapped into a backward fist. Some more powerful sorcerers, those more thoroughly possessed by the Devourers, could manifest terrible feats at will. Intuition and experience told the old man that this witch was not of that caliber.

"Go on then," spat the witch. "Git it done, then."

"The rules here are real simple like. Tell me where my boy is and I let you die."

The witch tried to spit blood. In its weakness it mostly drooled down its own chin, but the sentiment was clear. She would need more persuasion. The old man twisted his blade, shredding the witch's intestines more thoroughly.

"You dodged me in Emerald, bitch, but I've got you now. I've spent the last month tracking you down. I got no qualms about spending a few more days twisting answers outta you."

The old man's words were true. For months now he had been tracking down and slaying witches and native shamans. Even suspect members of the proper clergy had met his blade. Any poor bastard with a tie to anything occult drew the old man's attention and his wrath.

Impotent rage filled the witch's bloodshot eyes. The old man imagined that his victim's mind was calling out to those that came before. This thought didn't scare him, as experience had taught him that prayers were a one-sided affair.

Not foolish enough to turn his back on an enemy, the old man took a few backward steps and knelt by his pack. Eyes still locked on the witch, he reached into his bag, retrieving his papers and tobacco.

"What's your name, witch?"

"... Fiona," the witch whispered, after a pause that was caused by either pain or reluctance.

"The name your folks gave you. Not your whore name, or your witch name."

"Fiona's my born name. I ain't ashamed. Got no need to hide who I am."

"Well, Fiona, believe it or not, I don't much like hurtin' folk. I'm an old hand at it, and I'm good at it. Don't take no pleasure in it, though. And I reckon you don't much like the feeling of that steel in your guts. So let's make this easy, huh?"

The old man rolled a cigarette as he spoke, but stayed vigilant of the witch.

"Where's my son, Fiona?"

With much effort, the witch forced a smile and glared right into the old man's eyes.

"Thurs done took your boy. Ain't no getting him back."

"Getting him back is my concern. You just tell me where to find Thurs."

"Thurs walks the road to the future. The path paved with blood and gold."

One weakness the old man had noticed in most "learned men," be they witches or lawyers, was they all fancied themselves more clever than everyone else. And while Fiona had tried to hide the truth in a vague puzzle, the old man at once understood. It made perfect sense.

Satisfied with Fiona's cooperation, the old man removed the gladius from the witch's gut, allowing diseased, black blood to bubble out from the wound. With the sword now free, he delivered a fierce chopping blow that severed the witch's head from its body and ejected its corrupt spirit from the empirical world.

CHAPTER TWO

Dark thoughts enveloped Emmett's mind, like devouring shadows consuming all light. His mother's hollow cough, that persistent and slow rattle of her inevitable death, seemed as loud and real in his ears as if he were at her death bed rather than a quarter mile from home. He could see her ashy, sunken eyes and her taut cheeks—the stretched parchment cheeks of a mummy.

Set just beneath and parallel to his sorrowful preoccupation with his ill Ma, anger bubbled and roiled. Emmett's anger was powerful and deep. It was an emotion far more pronounced than any sixteen-year-old boy should have to contend with. The causes of his inner rage were legion, but this day his anger was focused on a single source. Mackum.

Mackum was an orange farmer who owned several acres a few miles out from town. The farmer had found use in Emmett's strength and size. The kid was not just big for his age, he was a monstrous boy who towered nearly a head above anyone in town now that his Pa was gone. Despite Emmett's usefulness to Mackum, the farmer made no secret of the fact that Emmett's very existence offended him. This never stopped Mackum from hiring him in harvest season. If Emmett wanted his five cents per sack, though, he had to listen to Mackum's bullshit about how he was an abomination and how no white man in his right mind would bed an Injun.

Somewhere below the ethereal coughing of his mother Emmett could hear Mackum calling him redskin and savage. The farmer's disgusted, judgmental gaze burned from behind the mental images of his mother. His mother's loving gaze dissolved into Mackum's hateful, baneful eyes. This mental imagery angered Emmett even more, reminding him on some unconscious level that a bastard like Mackum would continue to live and prosper, while his kind-hearted Ma would die in pain. All the worse, she would pass on without seeing his Pa ever again. Unless the war were to end in the next week perhaps.

***

The ragged breathing from the other room, while barely audible, struck Emmett's ears like the most ominous thunder. He tried to focus on his task, cooking up a chicken soup to ease his mother's discomfort, but all he could think was that each weak cough and labored breath was another clomp of the pale horse's hooves. While Emmett's mind was captured by the fear of his mother's impending end, his soup began to boil over, spilling broth into the flames below.

Emmett shook the thoughts of doom from his mind and focused on stirring the boiling soup. The consumption, if that's what it was, may have been taking his mother away soon, but he had to focus on how he could make her comfortable today. With his father on the other side of the country, nearly a continent away from Affirmation, California, it was his job to take care of his mother, their home, and the family business. Emmett was nearly sixteen, a grown man by the standards of the west, but he knew he wasn't ready to be the man of the house. Sure, he was strong enough, a bull for his age, and he could handle himself in a brawl, but tending to the needs of a dying woman was beyond his skill set. With his mother too sick to take on any seamstress work, the weight of financial responsibility lay solely on Emmett as well.

When his father had left for the war, their family gunsmithing business had been lucrative and bustling. California knew no shortage of people looking for quality iron. Things this far west weren't quite as civilized as in the soft-bellied east. A man couldn't depend on the law out here. He had to have the means and will to take care of his own. Unfortunately, Emmett lacked the level of skill that his father had with firearms. He knew the basics well enough, and kept a minimal amount of cash coming in, but he was incapable of creating the deadly works of art that had earned his father such respect. Men would come from miles around to commission one-of-a-kind pistols, uniquely named in the tradition of ancient smiths. That part of the business had dried up after Emmett's few failed attempts to recreate his father's work. Now he mostly made ammunition for folks, and worked part-time picking oranges for that obnoxious bastard, Mackum.

Emmett pulled the pot away from the fire and placed it on a stone slat in the middle of the kitchen table. He picked a bowl out from the cupboard, a plain clay piece adorned with orange and brown designs of the Paiute tribe. He smiled, remembering painting the bowl with his mother as a child. She would tell him the legends and tales of her own father's people, while they painted in the angular style of her ancestors. Emmett's father would grumble his disapproval, but never actively tried to stop it. His mother's interest in the native side of her ancestry had always been too intertwined with superstition for his father's liking. Emmett's old man had always cautioned against belief in anything greater than black powder and American ingenuity.

He filled the bowl that he and his mother had designed with a brothy soup that would hopefully ease her coughing. It smelled like chicken soup all right, but somehow didn't taste the same as the stuff his mother used to cook. He hoped she wouldn't notice the poor craftsmanship of his cooking. If he was only a quarter the gunsmith his father was, then he was only a tenth the cook that his mother was.

It was hard for him to look at her. As long as he could remember, his mother had been beautiful, healthy, and full of life. Her black silken hair was still well maintained—Emmett would comb it for her twice a day—but it had acquired a much more silver tone over the last few months. The piercing gaze of her brown eyes, so full of strength, now seemed defeated by sickness. Her lithe and strong body had atrophied and left a shriveling shell in its place. While her dark features contrasted against his father's Nordic pedigree, her strength had always matched his—both in body and spirit. Now his father was gone and his mother was fading into nothingness.

"I made you a light soup, Ma. I know you haven't got much appetite, but it might settle your cough a bit." Emmett kept his voice low but enthusiastic.

"Thank you, baby. Can you get me my tray?" Emmett's mother whispered the words, trying to sit herself up in bed. Tremors rocked her whole body as she coughed, before settling into a sitting position against a large pillow behind her. Emmett frowned, his mother's coughs sending shivers through his own body as well.

He grabbed a small wooden tray, a simple, flat piece of hickory about a yard by a foot, and placed it across his mother's lap. She nodded her thanks, and Emmett placed the bowl of soup on the tray. As she looked down and took note of the bowl he had chosen, a genuine smile crossed the lips of the dying woman.

"Do you remember when we made this, Emmett?" his mother asked in a raspy voice.

"I sure do, Ma. You told me how the symbols brought good luck. Thought we could use some of that luck about now."

"Good thing your Pa ain't around to hear that kinda talk," Emmett's mother laughed. The laugh descended into a labored hacking.

Despite his mother's words, Emmett did wish his father were there to scold him for seeking out luck from a painted bowl. He wanted his father to walk through the door with a real-world way to save his mother's life. He wanted to hear that gravelly voice tell him that everything was going to be okay. That wasn't going to happen though. He was on his own.

Emmett's mother could read the dark expression in his gray-blue eyes. It was almost as if she could read his mind.

"You're a fine man, Emmett. You're doing your best for both of us." She paused, trying to stifle a cough. "I know you think your father could stop this if he was here, but he couldn't."

The boy, who was now man of the house, closed his eyes, trying not to cry.

"I'd go as far as saying you're handling this better than your Pa would if he was here. He's a damn good man, but facing a problem he couldn't out-think or out-shoot would drive him mad. I'd be having to take care of him if he saw me like this."

A single tear streaked down Emmett's face, causing his cheeks to flush with anger at his own weakness.

"No. Pa would find a way. He'd fight God and the devil themselves if he had to."

"Emmett, baby, sometimes there just isn't an answer. Sometimes it's braver to end a song than to write another verse."

***

It was nighttime now, and Emmett stood in the kitchen alone. His mother was fast asleep in her bedroom, and Emmett was putting away the dishes he had cleaned after dinner. His mother was getting worse, and her willingness to submit to oblivion hurt and angered him. The talk about his father had stirred up emotions he tried to keep buried most of the time—feelings of abandonment and anger battled against respect and love in the young man's tumultuous mindscape.

He missed his Pa something fierce, and was so proud that he had gone to stand up against the Union dictators, but damn it, Emmett was mad. How could he leave them here? Wasn't family more important than Davis or Lincoln, or some imaginary line in a country they had stolen anyway? Wouldn't it be nobler to stay and watch his boy become a man than to go kill the sons of others?

But deep in his heart, Emmett believed his father was right. Lincoln's thugs were crushing freedom and dissent all the way out here, where they had no business telling folks what to do or think. Word was that Confederate sympathizers in Virginia City had been taken to Fort Churchill and locked away, all for simply speaking their minds. It was that kind of blatant tyranny that had forced Emmett's father to head for Texas and take up arms for the South. The West, and all of America really, was about freedom and independence. The actions of the Union had demonstrated that they had clearly forgotten those ideals.

As thoughts of his father and the familial duty he had shirked in lieu of some grandiose national duty bounced around Emmett's mind, the young man placed the bowl that he and his mother had painted back in the cupboard. As he pulled his hand away, he paused to admire the simple angular designs of muted, rusty tones that reflected so much of California itself. The symbols meant something, but he didn't quite understand what. His mother had explained them as good luck charms, but Emmett believed that was an oversimplified explanation. There seemed to be something deeper in their shapes ... something powerful.

With one finger, Emmett traced one of the symbols—a diamond of yellow ochre set over a rust-colored rectangle. He imagined the power of the land itself being channeled through the symbol and into his body. Broken fragments of legends his mother had told him flooded his mind. Shamans speaking to the dead and glimpsing images of the future through dancing flames. Braves calling upon the spirits of bears and raptors to give them strength and courage. Warriors blessed by ancient spirits who could walk through volleys of arrows and gunfire unharmed.

Doctors, three of them in fact, had failed to provide any substantial treatment for his mother. The tonics and cure-alls of the white man were doing little to even comfort her. American ingenuity, for all it was worth, had failed Emmett. Perhaps his father would be bright enough to find a reasoned means of saving his mother's life, but Emmett wasn't the man his father was. Emmett was barely a man at all.

If neither the white man's science nor the white man's God could fix things (and yes, Emmett had prayed at length to the God of Israel), then perhaps older, forgotten solutions could be unearthed. Emmett knew that the stories of his grandmother's tribe may well be the nonsense that his father insisted. Hell, he doubted that his mother even believed them, but if there was a chance they held any kernel of truth, didn't he owe it to his family to at least investigate them? If some Paiute medicine man, maybe even his own grandfather, held the secret to conquering his mother's illness, was it not Emmett's duty to secure that secret? And honestly, what did he have to lose?

Emmett put the rest of the dishes away and headed to his own bedroom, comforted by the thought that he at least had one more possibility to save his mother's life. In the morning he would pay one of the ladies in town to keep an eye on his mother, and then he would take his mule south to the Paiute reservation. At a good clip, he could be there in three hours, and back home before dark.

For the first time since his mother had taken ill, Emmett slept soundly through the night.

CHAPTER THREE

When the witch named Fiona had pointed him to the "path paved with blood and gold," the old man was certain that Thurs must be somehow tied to the Overland Route. The railroad was almost a deity unto itself. A good deal of money and blood had been sacrificed to it. The vision of the steel tracks brought ideas of salvation, escape, and hope to an entire nation. Men devoted their lives to its service. It made perfect sense that Thurs would be uniquely interested in the birth of a new god. Strangely, the old man found no hatred in his heart at the thought of the railroad as a god. If he were to get behind a god, it would be one like that—a deity that man had created and that man could control. That was far more palatable to him than some unfathomable alien—no matter their agenda.

Traveling from the Mexican border, where he had ended Fiona's life, the old man made his way to Oakland, California. From there, the tired Confederate traced the Central Pacific from its origin point, in search of the thing that stole his son. From Oakland on, the trail was wrought with greed, corruption, and death, but of a distinctly human nature. Shady backroom deals were made. Workers suffered. Men made their fortunes or were swindled out of their savings. No arcane influence seemed to be at work though. Even the Celestial rail workers, with their strange customs, seemed untouched by the Devourers.

When he arrived at Donner Summit, a gorgeous mountain pass above a lake that shared the same namesake, the old man realized that the efforts of the last few months had been a waste. The procession of the railroad was brought to a near standstill here. Workers labored day and night to blast tunnels through the miles of ancient stone. Black powder and nitroglycerin kept the project going, but at an excruciatingly slow pace. If Thurs was somehow manipulating the railroad, it was on the side of the competing Union Pacific company, far across the Sierra Nevada.

This left the old man with a choice that might have been difficult for others. He could sacrifice several more weeks and seek a route around the mountain range, or he could cross the inhospitable land on foot, in the middle of December. While he was patient, the old man still understood the value of every second. With that in mind, there was only one real option, and the old man wasn't prone to wasting time on lamentations of "what ifs." Without a moan or complaint the old man continued east.

Snow was falling in the Sierra Nevada Mountains, creating a monochrome landscape of white powder set against gray stone. The old man didn't care for snow, and he had hoped to have seen it for the last time in '65. He had long ago come to terms with the fact that whatever powers moved this world often had plans at odds with his own. This was just the way of things, and it was not the old man's nature to dwell on setbacks. His mind was singularly set on one goal, and roadblocks were only there to be smashed. With silent determination, the old man made his way across the rocky mountain path and through the snow-laden winds.

It would be hard to hunt or trap any food during the Sierra winter. Game would be scarce, and the seasons of gathering lay behind and ahead. Anticipating the struggles that lay before him, he had bartered for several weeks of rations with the rail boss at Donner's Pass.

Mostly he had gotten stale bread and smoked venison, paying for it with gold that was worth ten times the value of the food. As for clothes, he'd managed to rustle up a few garments that he could layer beneath what he already wore. There seemed to be nothing warmer for an overcoat than the worn, dirty, Confederate artillery coat that he'd been living in for so many years now. It would get him through most of his trek across the mountains. That was what mattered— keeping momentum toward the goal. Obstacles like hunger or frostbite would have to be dealt with as they came up.

The journey across the mountains was unpleasant at the best of times. Temperatures dropped to well below freezing at night, and on the warmest days the old man's breath still danced visibly in the air. Little could be found in the way of shelter or dry wood, leaving the old man to depend on his bulky layers and his hatred to keep him warm most nights. Additionally, the old man was fatiguing far easier than he had ever before in his life. He wondered if his age was finally catching up with him, or if one of the witches he had sent to the grave had laid some manner of dying curse upon him.

After three weeks of trekking down snow-flooded wagon roads, surviving on meager rations and sleeping beneath lean-tos on frozen ground, the old man began to second-guess his decision. He was unsure of how much ground he had traveled, but he was sure it wasn't much. In the last week the path hard hardened, and he now walked on packed, frozen snow, rather than through knee-deep powder or slush. His momentum should have increased but, now that the landscape had become more agreeable, his body had become less so. Maybe a path around the mountains would have delivered him to the Union Pacific rails with greater rapidity.

Skirting the Sierra Nevada would have been a more sure course at the very least. If the icy winds and unforgiving snow stole the life from him, he would be of no use to his boy. And were the frigid winter winds not the ally of Thurs? The old man had no facts to back up this assertion, but he knew it in his heart that the deathly winter was a tool of the Devourers, just as all primal forces and peoples were their tools.

Lost in his thoughts, tired and aching from the cold, the old man didn't notice that snow in front of him looked to be of a less firm nature. Taking a step, he meant to place his right foot upon the packed snow, but instead went through it. With more sleep and better food he could have easily pushed himself back onto more solid ground with his other leg. His muscles had betrayed him, however, in protest to the cold, abuse, and lack of fuel. Like some great, clumsy child, the old man tumbled headlong into the soft snow before him. His great weight, both from his own massive frame as well as the gear he carried, forced him deep into the cold snow. The freezing powder cushioned his fall, but collapsed atop him as well, invading every opening his clothing left vulnerable. His face stung as thousands of unique crystals stole the warmth from his flesh.

Adrenaline was pumping, but the cold and weariness still made it hard for the old man to flip onto his back. Once he accomplished this seemingly Sisyphean task, he was greeted by more snow to the face. He was unsure how much of the powder had collapsed onto him, but found himself more annoyed than worried. Light still made its way through the snow, and he guessed he could be no more than a yard and a half buried.

That was until he tried to get up. With each struggle to gain his feet or pull himself up, the white seemed to suck him down further. Like arctic quick sand, it refused to loosen its grip. The old man struggled angrily and found himself descending further.

The strange sensation that he was being sucked down beyond the snow's natural depth gave credence to what he had been thinking only a few moments before. This primal place, away from mankind's will and reason, was well within the power of Thurs and the mad, devouring titans of Utgard.

With the snow in his eyes, and the light above fading, the old man was unable to see. Nonetheless, he was confident that talons, formed from ice and snow, had grasped onto his clothes and limbs. His mind screamed for his muscles to fight harder but, even as he urged his body on, the cold sapped his strength. Finally the frost invaded his mouth and nose, drowning the lone soldier in frozen water. Unable to breathe, his body out of fight, the old man cursed and screamed until the light of consciousness expired. Darkness and cold eclipsed his burning rage and the old man drifted into Hel.

CHAPTER FOUR

Once, the whole of what the white men had named California and Nevada were the hunting grounds and the home of the Paiute tribe. Now, the descendants of the men and women who had roamed these lands since the Great Spirit first breathed life into the world were crowded onto a chunk of lifeless soil only eight thousand acres large.

Bishop Colony. It was this open-sky prison, barren of hope yet overflowing with disease, addiction, and apathy, that Emmett's grandfather called home. The angry and distrustful stares that the residents there cast him were further proof that he was not a child of two cultures, but a twin pariah. The folks in town looked down on his family, despite the respect his father had earned as a master craftsman. His father's finest work couldn't wash away the rusty tint of Emmett's flesh or the raven silk of his hair. The same went for the more distinctive native features that his mother displayed.

Shortly after riding into Bishop Colony, Emmett stopped his mule near a couple of children who were looking upon him with both fear and excitement. The two boys, maybe around eight or nine years old, had been playing outside of a tiny hut made from sticks and straw. They could not take their dark eyes off of him. Emmett's cotton shirt, blue jeans, and hard-soled leather boots must have seemed so alien to these two boys who were dressed in simple clothes made from deer skin and yucca fiber. For all Emmett knew, he was the closest thing to a white man they had ever seen.

From the few Paiute he had seen so far, he was about a head taller than any of the grown men, having inherited his height from his old man. He could see how his size might intimidate the Paiute children. On the other hand, he guessed that they didn't get many visitors, so even some giant mongrel riding a comically small mule would be a joy to see.

"I'm looking for the elder shaman. A man named Poohwi." Emmett spoke the words in a pleasant voice, trying to put the children at ease.

The two boys looked at Emmett for a moment in silence, before simultaneously breaking into a chatter of indiscernible language. *Of course*, Emmett thought, *they don't speak a lick of English.*

A deeper voice, that of an adult, issued some strange word from inside the hut. It sounded like some manner of command. Judging by the way the children immediately ran back into the hut, it was just that. As the children ran into the small home, a grown man stepped out through the open doorway of the hut. The man, whose hard, angular face held eyes the color of rich topsoil, regarded Emmett coolly.

"Poohwi is not taking visitors, stranger."

"I get it. You don't fancy outsiders. I really can't leave without seeing him though."

"I'm afraid that's impossible," the man from Bishop Colony said in a slow, deliberate manner. "Poohwi is quite sick. Any excitement could be detrimental to his health."

"His daughter—my mother—is dying. The white man's medicine is failing her. I need his help."

The man before Emmett paused, looking him up and down. Emmett felt as if the man was looking through his physical form and into his very soul. The thought made him vaguely uncomfortable.

"I can think of no better gift for a dying man than the chance to save his child. I will take you to your grandfather."

Minutes later, the Paiute man, who introduced himself as Taba, walked with Emmett, guiding him to the home of Poohwi. As they traveled deeper into the reservation, Emmett became acutely aware that the looks that the Paiute were shooting him were worse than what he had experienced in his own town. At least the white men were cultured enough to try to conceal their disdain. The Paiute took no such measures. This half-breed dressed in the clothes of the invaders was not welcome or trusted. Looking around, he could hardly blame them for their anger and distrust. Cultured society had really left them with the short end of the stick. Still, an understanding of their dislike was not enough to make Emmett feel at ease. He kept riding through, careful not to make eye contact with anyone.

It was nearly dusk as Emmett and Taba approached the straw hovel where Poohwi laid his head at night. Celestial pigments— orange, pink, and purple—mingled across the horizon. The tiny homes of the native people stood like solid shadows against the brilliant sunset.

A smoky smell of some unfamiliar spice wafted out from the shelter. While the scent was not inherently unpleasant, the alien fragrance did little to settle Emmett's already nervous belly. He knew little of his mother's family, but was aware that she had not spoken to her father in many, many years. Exactly what had caused the schism between father and daughter was unclear. But Emmett was certain there would still be some bad blood.

"This is as far as I go. Settle your business and be on your way, please." Taba's tone was unfriendly, but not aggressive. He seemed to wish Emmett no ill will. It was clear, however, that he didn't want the young man on Paiute land any longer than absolutely necessary.

While Emmett's mother had shared many beliefs and customs of her people with him, she had never discussed common day-to-day practices, like the customary way to announce oneself for a visit. Should he just knock, or announce himself? Should he just walk in?

Finally Emmett walked up to the doorless entryway and cast his voice into the modest shelter.

"Poohwi? May I come in?"

No answer.

Emmett spoke up again. "My name is Emmett. I'm Kylie Wongraven's son. Or Kylie Brunelle, I guess. She took her Ma's name, right?

The only response from within was a fit of dry coughing. Once the coughing subsided, Emmett spoke again.

"I think you called her Uweka."

Another cough, more brief this time, sounded forth from the dark confines of the straw home. Then finally a response.

"Uweka?" the voice of his grandfather weakly asked in response.

Emmett crouched and edged into the hut, fighting back some illogical fear that chilled him. Something about the tone of Poohwi's sickly voice did not sit right with him. Despite the weakness in the wheezing, breathy intonation of that single word, Emmett could hear something subtly strong and dark within Poohwi's voice.

More than just the whispery malignance of his grandfather's voice struck a bad chord with Emmett. The shadowy confines of the tiny building contained a darkness so deep and voluminous that it seemed to repel the waning light of the sunset and defy the limitations of the space within the hut. Of course, these were crazy ideas, and Emmett pushed them as far into the back of his mind as he could manage.

After a few seconds his eyes adjusted to the darkness of his grandfather's home. He couldn't make out any details, but he could distinguish the vague shape of an old man lying atop a bed of hay. His features were shrouded, but deeply ingrained wrinkles crisscrossed the skin on Poohwi's face, and his dark eyes were sunken deep into their sockets.

Other objects stood out, looking sinister in the darkness. A stone knife, which was probably no more than a household tool, invoked visions of ritual murder under fading light. A long pipe, carved from the bone of some animal and decorated with feathers, still held the burning, orange embers of some arcane herb in its bowl. Hanging above Poohwi's bed was what Emmett could only think of as a mobile of various animal bones, for that he could glean no practical purpose, but conjured a dozen nightmare functions in his mind.

Emmett swallowed down his fear, thinking it best not to waste the sick geriatric's time.

"I know you're sick, and I don't wanna make you any more uncomfortable than you are, but I need your help." Emmett sucked in a deep breath, trying to work up the will to say the words he knew and could not speak. "My mother's dying."

"Uweka?" Again Poohwi replied with a question. Emmett wondered if the old shaman was in his right mind.

"Medicine's failed her. The doctors we've seen can't make her better. I prayed to Christ, but if he's there he ain't listening."

A terrible and pained laugh crept out through the shaman's withered lips.

"So you seek answers from the world she left behind? From the tribe she left to rot?" Poohwi's words were pure venom.

"I don't know what happened with you and her and her mother. All I know is that I can't let my ma die and I hope you can't let your daughter die."

Poohwi grunted, then broke into another coughing fit. Emmett waited for a response after the coughing had stopped, but was met with only silence.

"I can hear death in your voice. The reaper is coming for you too. You have the chance to do something good before you go, though. I know you can save her. If you can't, then I have shit for options."

Another moment of silence passed. Emmett tried to push back the flood of emotion he was feeling and stem the tide of oncoming tears. Finally Poohwi made a sound as if coming to the conclusion of a series of mental calculations.

"You are right, boy," Poohwi hissed in a breathless voice. "I can make a difference before I go. And I should."

Poohwi pointed toward a basket near his feet. It was woven straw with painted designs that most likely were bright and colorful in the daylight, but took on a monochromatic tone in the darkness.

"Bring me a hide from that basket. Also, my knife."

Emmett did not question his mother's sire. He brought the knife and hide over to Poohwi without a word.

The shaman sat up as best he could. He laid the hide across his lap and called Emmett closer.

"For all things there are prices," Poohwi whispered. "For this, the price is blood."

He then reached out and clasped onto Emmett's enormous hand. There was a feebleness to the old shaman's grip.

"Are you willing to bleed for your mother?"

Emmett was scared. The entirety of the situation was becoming too much for him—the darkness, the sickly old shaman, the primitive stone knife. Nonetheless, he mumbled in the affirmative and allowed Poohwi to slice open his palm.

Pain shot through Emmett's body as the razor-sharp flint of Poohwi's blade cut across his palm. Blood pooled up from the wound, looking like ink in the shadows of the hovel.

"You may actually have the nerve for what comes next, you bear of a boy."

Without saying another word, Poohwi began to draw, in Emmett's blood, a crude map across the piece of hide. The map would lead Emmett to an ancient place, one of the first bits of creation to come out of the nothingness before. A place too secret and mystical for the white men to discover on their own.

"There is a magic that can help you. A magic that can save her. But like this map I give you to find it, the magic itself will have a price."

The sickly old Paiute dipped his finger into the blood pooled in Emmett's palm again, letting the crimson life force coat his wrinkled finger.

"What are you willing to pay for your mother's life?"

Emmett wasn't sure if his grandfather was offering a stern warning, testing his devotion, or having a go at scaring the half-breed. Poohwi's motivations did not matter to him. His answer was the same, regardless.

"Anything."

***

There is a tendency in children and teenagers to confuse the hierarchy of troubles that they face. Three days had passed since Emmett had left the Paiute reservation. He was short on food and water. The nights were getting colder the deeper east he went. And now he stood at the narrow entrance to a hidden cave at the foot of the Sierra Nevada. He had come to retrieve some ancient knowledge that a bitter, crazed shaman had warned would carry a steep price. The most pressing trouble in his mind, however, was how he would pay Mary Coughlin for the extra days she was taking care of his mother.

The bright light of day seemed to barely penetrate the first few feet within the unassuming cave's entrance. Despite the darkness within, Emmett could make out the carving on the stone floor, just as his grandfather had described it. A sigil that looked vaguely like a crooked, broken cross was cut smoothly into the rough stone floor. There seemed to be a glow to it, like sunlit stained-glass set within bedrock. Although the crooked cross was hidden adequately within the shadows, once Emmett's attention fell upon it, the symbol seemed to shine like the sun, or a burst of captured lightning.

Perhaps if he had been a fully grown man, in mind and body, then his sense of trouble would have been more refined. As an adult, there would have been a good chance that Emmett would never have stepped into the *Cavern of the First Breath*. Being a desperate, teenage boy, Emmett suffered from an overabundance of bravery and under-abundance of sense.

Oswald, the mule that had served as transport for his journey, whinnied and pulled at his tether. The animal sensed something there that it did not like. Emmett feared that Oswald might have caught scent of a bear or a mountain cat. If such a thing was lurking within the cave he would be in a tough spot. Poohwi had assured him that no animal would care to call this subterranean place home. If the shaman's words were true, then whatever bad feeling the mule was getting must have some esoteric reason.

Having been raised by a practical man for most of his life, Emmett found less fear in the idea of some ancient slumbering evil than he did a young, slumbering predator.

The young man lit a torch, little more than stick of hickory lathered in tar, and pressed into the darkness of the cave. The mouth of the cave was short and narrow. Emmett had to stoop and tuck his arms in front of him in order to fit. Despite the discomfort of the tight quarters, Emmett took special care not to step upon the engraving of the crooked cross. To do so felt wrong and fundamentally dangerous.

The darkness of the cave seemed to be drawn to Emmett, reacting to some manner of gravity within his soul. The torch kept the hungry shadows at bay, but only by the smallest margin. In such tight quarters, that small margin was enough. Emmett could make out the stone earth directly ahead of him, which was the most important detail to see. If some beast had made this place home, though, Emmett wouldn't see it break into the light until it was far too late. There would be just enough time to catch a glimpse of his killer before being mauled.

The calcified stone walls that scraped against his shoulder were also illuminated and, to Emmett's dismay, they seemed to be narrowing even further. Emmett feared that someone of his size may just get jammed between the walls and stuck in the cave forever. For his mother's sake, he pushed on.

After what had felt like an hour to his stooped back and cramping muscles, the narrowing corridor opened up into a massive grotto with stone ceilings high enough to rival the cathedral he'd seen as a boy one time in Los Angeles. The corridor that he passed through stood ten feet above the dark lake. Emmett had nearly fallen out from the narrow walkway and into the grotto, but managed to catch himself at the last moment.

A moss of some sort, alive with a soft glow of its own, bathed the underground lake in a soft, emerald glow. Pale, yellow stalactites hung down, like the overbite of some awful titan. In the middle of the cavern, amidst the pool of black, shimmering water, four steps rose from below the surface and ended before a wide, stone block painted with dark, runny stains. Draped over the block, Emmett could see dozens of hides, all decorated with exotic writing.

Emmett could not imagine trying to get undressed in the claustrophobic confines of the tunnel. Instead he threw his fear of the oncoming night's cold to the wind and leapt into the lake fully clothed. The torch he left behind, to burn within the stone corridor and mark the way he had entered.

His substantial mass made a large splash as his body tore through the surface tension of the water. He did not know how far down the lakebed might be, but his body had found no sign of it thus far, and he was not interested in discovering that secret. The deep, incredible cold of the lake sent the young man's muscles into shock, freezing them in place. Below the surface of the water all light seemed to disappear and Emmett could feel the slimy tendrils of some unseen creature grabbing at him. He began to panic, and sucked in a mouthful of water before successfully swimming up and breaching the surface.

With his head above the surface, Emmett coughed up the salty water of the black grotto. Only after he had finished coughing and choking did he realize that the lake seemed to be made up of salt water. He wondered how the far off Pacific was contributing to such a place, but the question vanished just as quickly as it had come about. There were more pressing mysteries at hand.

Emmett rolled his shoulders and his neck, his chin grazing the rippling surface of the frigid water. His muscles were screaming in protest against the cold, but the boy commanded them to fall in line. A moment later he began swimming toward the steps that rose up like the ruins of a flooded city.

Soaked and dripping, Emmett clambered up the steps once his limbs found purchase upon them. Climbing up was hard, as the steps were covered in calcium and algae. He slipped more than once and managed to cut his hand open, from the base of his palm the base of his pinky finger, on a barnacle that clung to the partially submerged staircase. After a few tries and much cursing, Emmett finally made it up the steps.

The stone slab was only feet away from him. Up close, the runny stains on the stone that he had spotted from afar reminded him of the rust colored rivulets that ran down the side of the butcher's block in his kitchen. Images from the penny-dreadfuls that his friend, Oliver, had sometimes let him borrow came to the forefront of his mind—stories of sinister blood sacrifices and pagan cults.

That wasn't quite right. Emmett knew in his bones that this was not a chamber of sacrifice. No, his first comparison to the butcher's block was more on point. This grotto was a place of feeding. Not for a mountain cat or bear either. No, it was the thing that first breathed the world into being who supped in this watery cavern. Emmett was sure of it.

His attention turned toward the numerous hides draped across the grotto's altar. He couldn't rightly tell what manner of animal they had come from, but each was finely tanned and covered in arcane symbols and geometric diagrams.

The language was alien to him, but there seemed to be a terrible power to it—some ancient force captured within the lines and shapes.

Fear began to overtake the young man, forcing adrenaline into his veins and causing his usually calm hands to shake. He needed to get out. Now. The only way he could see in or out of the cave was marked by the light of his torch, and that path was a man and a half above the water line.

The terrible realization that he had literally jumped into a possibly inescapable situation increased Emmett's panic. His head whipped back and forth, scanning for any means of egress. There was none. The eerie glow of the moss and the teasing light from his torch visually impressed upon him the hopelessness of his situation.

He was alone. Alone with the gentle, mocking lapping of the sea against the ancient stone walls, and the crackling laughter of his torch high above. Alone with whatever primordial creatures may lurk in the water surrounding him. Alone with whatever hungry ghosts may haunt the stone walls and stale, salty air.

But there was something else. There was the altar. And there were the hides, with their ancient secrets. If the hides could unlock the power that his grandfather had spoken of, if they could save his mother's life from sickness, then perhaps they could save him now.

Emmett turned back to the altar and picked up one of the hides. His selection was not random. Somehow the young man knew that the spells drawn upon this piece of tanned flesh, the same chestnut color as Poohwi's skin, would hold the key to his survival.

Once his left hand touched the hide, the blood that dripped from his sliced palm was pulled into the leathery substrate. This ancient text, which must have been sealed with oil or wax (for it showed no sign of water damage), soaked in the crimson life force as hungrily as a dry, cotton rag. It did more than just absorb it. It sucked and slurped at it, demanding and crying and screaming for more.

The world began to sway in front of Emmett's eyes and he could feel his knees giving way. His body was weakening, as if it had been besieged by a hundred leeches. The sigils and seals and shapes on the hide began to take on a soft, pink glow. That soft glow became more intense and shifted to a deeper red. Emmett was reminded of how the veins of a bat's wings might take on an illuminated look if sunlight were to filter through the leathery gliders.

Before he had time to dwell on the thought for very long, he saw that he was looking at the ceiling, and its perspective was shifting rapidly. It was as if the room was spinning around him. Soon he feared the water would slap him in the back and drag his body deep within its cold embrace.

Then the words came to him. The sheet of flesh with the glowing figures was no longer in his field of vision, but he now knew what those figures said. He knew, as if some other voice were speaking them in his mind. And at least a little bit, he understood the power behind those words.

As gravity continued to shift around him and the sea pushed past his back, Emmett opened his mouth and began to speak the words that would save his life and damn his soul. The words that would give him everything he wanted and take away everything he had. The alien incantation, nearly unpronounceable, came out loud, clear, and powerful, even as the cold water of the Pacific filled his mouth and lungs.

CHAPTER FIVE

Ice cracked beneath the wheels of the cannon as its position was adjusted. The old man couldn't hear the shrill breaking sound over the roar of battle, but felt it through the soles of his boots. The hefty bronze weapon did not roll easily on the frozen ground. He found it miraculous that it moved at all, even with his massive strength behind it. It was as if the ice itself had grabbed ahold of the wheels and fought against his attempts to move it. This concept seemed familiar to him in a faraway manner, but now was not the time to ponder feelings of déjà vu.

The enemy was closing in, more quickly than he liked. If there had been another man or two to help move the damn cannon he might have stood a chance, but he was the last living soul in the Confederate battalion. The corpses of his brothers watched him with the marked disinterest of the deceased. The approaching giant—a terrible creature with pale blue skin, onyx hair, and the blue uniform of the Northern army—observed his struggle with the sadistic amusement of a confident predator.

Without needing to look behind him, the old man could sense the ice and snow, and the gray of winter encroaching upon the warm, vibrant landscape of his California home. He could feel the life being sucked from the sapling that he and his boy had planted. The crackling of living leaves turning brown and brittle filled his ears like thunder.

The cannon and he were the last lines of defense. The unnatural cold—the word fimblewinter kept entering his mind— would soon take his land, his home, and his family. Between him and the end of his world stood only a shining Howitzer, with its wheels stuck in the ice.

The approaching giant let out a massive howl from three hundred yards away. The sound was like creaking ice and breaking glass, followed by a gust of arctic wind. The giant's frozen breath hit the last standing Confederate like a sack of ice to the face. Black, necrotized tissue instantaneously replaced the rawhide skin of the old man's hands. The same icy burn gnawed at his face and ears, and the old man was sure that his head bore the same frostbite as his digits. Near him, a Southern battle flag stiffened and shattered from the power of the eldritch scream. The frost-covered bits of the Stars and Bars danced away on the evil winds.

Knowing that all he held dear was on the verge of annihilation, the soldier put all his strength and will into pushing the Howitzer into position. The icy grip of the treasonous ground released, allowing the cannon to be swung in a wide arc and pointed at the giant. The creature threw its enormous head back and let out a shrill laugh that was incongruous with its titanic form.

"Laugh it up, Yank," the old man muttered as he adjusted the angle of his weapon.

Confident of his mark, the old man fired the bronze gun, loosing a ball of fiery lead toward the ice-skinned invader. The shot missed its mark by a yard on the left. A curse escaped the old man's lips and he went about the slow business of loading his weapon.

No cannonballs remained, so he bent down, and, in desperation, tore the skull from one of his decomposing brothers-in-arms. The wind whistled through its empty eyes and the old man could have sworn that it sounded like a somber, mocking version of the melody from Laurel Lee. This disturbed him more than reason called for, and, with more than a little bit of fear, he forced the skull into the barrel of the Howitzer.

The thunderclaps of the approaching giant were getting louder. The monster was close. If the old man didn't act fast and effectively, it would devour everything in this world that was worth a damn.

Taking a deep breath, trying hard to block out the pain of his frostbitten skin, the old man fired another shot. The skull ejected from the cannon, trailed by flame and black smoke. This time it found its mark, and bore a hole straight through the chest of the Devourer. The wound showed no organs or vital bits inside. Rather, the giant looked like a wax figure whose chest had been burned through by a cigar.

After several long moments of pained disbelief, black ooze began filling the wound in the monster's chest. The massive creature fell to the earth and shattered like some crystal monolith. The resulting crash was louder than even the boom of the Howitzer, and the battlefield shook with the force from the fall. Careening from the dead, shattered hand of the Devourer was a massive cavalry sword, nearly the size of a grain silo. Like a nightmarish ice skate, the blade skidded along on its edge across the frozen plain. In its wake a deep groove was cut into the ice, revealing not soil or bedrock beneath, but rather a black, oozing substrate.

As the ichor of the diseased land bubbled up from its earthen wound, the broken shards of the Union titan began to take on a life of their own. Ranging in size from a pebble to well larger than a man, the pieces of the broken corpse began to form into devilish creatures with crystalline flesh and tattered uniforms, the color of the winter sky before dawn. There were hundreds of them, each armed with razor-sharp talons and gnashing stalactite teeth.

The old man could sense the fimblewinter behind him, encroaching further unto his home. The log fence that marked his property was creaking as the flash freeze caused the wood to contract with unnatural quickness. His grass was turning brown and then quickly fading to ashy grey.

It was more than just the cold threatening the old man's family and home. The swarm of monsters that had once been a god were storming forward, like a hateful, living hail storm. An insatiable compulsion to snuff out any and all life burned behind their eyes.

The old man had neither the bullets nor the time to shoot down each abomination. He would not allow these creatures to reach his wife and son. He would not let the cold northern winds capture his land. To the last drop of blood, he would fight these things.

There would be no time to reload the cannon, so the old man did the next best thing. With a strong kick, he knocked over the powder keg that stood near the Howitzer. Another push with his legs sent the barrel rolling toward the oncoming frost monsters.

The trollish creatures, dressed in the colors of the Union Army, took no notice of the rolling keg. Either their minds were incapable of self-preservation, or the implications of what was about to happen did not register in their alien brains.

The old man raised his revolver and leveled the sights on the barrel. Once the gap between the ice creatures and the keg had closed sufficiently, he pressed down on the cold steel trigger. The burning round cut through the frigid air like a runaway star. The old man's aim was true. A great blast of fire and force tore through the better number of monsters.

The shower of icy bits and melting crystalline limbs served as a testimony to the power held within the alchemy of man. Sulfur, saltpeter, and charcoal married through human ingenuity had proved enough to shatter the arcane binds of these things from beyond. That thought brought the slightest smirk to the old man's lips.

When the smoke cleared, the old man could see only seven trolls remaining. 'Seven is manageable,' he thought while training his irons on the closest monster. He aimed for the heart rather than the head, for even mindless creatures and animate machines have to circulate their fuel. He took in a deep inhalation of the frigid air, commanding his lungs to accept the burning cold oxygen. Clearing his mind of fear and hope and all things in between, the old man loosed one of his five remaining rounds. The bullet tore through the troll's chest, sending stress fractures through its entire torso. Midnight-blue ichor poured from the monster's wound as it fell backwards.

There was no pause among the other blizzard beasts. In their black eyes, a grim determination seemed to move them along, rather than mad rage. The old man reckoned that their unwavering ferocity came not from mindlessness, nor solely from rage, but from necessity. These creatures fought for their future, as he fought for his family. It was him or them—humanity or the devouring gods what lay beyond. They charged forward into death's valley because to waver meant oblivion.

The old man could respect this. He nonetheless continued to rain lead upon them. One shot for each monster, that's all he could afford. Swinging his iron to the leftmost target, he fired a single shot before ticking over to the next abomination. Four of the five bullets shot true and proper, destroying whatever pumps kept the vile life-stuff flowing through the children of Utgard. One shot strayed and blasted through the shoulder of its target. This was good enough for the old man. With only three remaining, he felt confident that his blade could finish the battle.

He pulled the thick, heavy sword from his belt. A comforting warmth radiated from its leather-wrapped grip. The warmth filled the old man with strength and pride. Like gunpowder, the gladius was a simple and elegant tool—something raw that had been harvested from the primal earth and shaped by will into an instrument of civilization. The warmth coming from the sword, he had no doubt, stemmed from the living will of mankind, of which he was both a contributor and a conduit.

With great effort, the old man forced the screaming muscles of his legs to power forward, despite the cold. With a shrieked battle cry, the old man charged at the three frost trolls. The trolls did not slow their pace, and met their enemy with a howl of their own. Seconds later, the first monster clashed with the old man.

With a vicious overhead strike, the old man slashed at his enemy. The troll let out a sickening, abomination of a laugh as it brought its arm up to deflect the blow. The horrible laughter was cut short as the gladius cleaved through the creature's forearm and continued down through its clavicle. The gladius was stuck in the beast's icy flesh. The old man kicked the creature hard in the chest while pulling his blade back. The force of the kick dislodged the weapon and shattered the monster's torso.

By this point, the second Union monster was upon him. This one was smaller than the last, half the old man's height, but quick as hell. With the speed and ferocity of a wild cat, the troll leaped on to the old man, knocking him back onto the icy battlefield. Its hands gripped around his massive neck, while its legs conformed to some unnatural position that allowed the beast to crouch on its enemy as it strangled.

The troll's mouth opened wide, revealing a maw full of razor-sharp flint and a black tongue that writhed like an eel. Still choking the old man with all of its unnatural might, the troll snapped its jaws in an attempt to tear the flesh from its quarry's face. With an agility that seemed supernatural for a man of his age and size, the old man brought the blade of his gladius between himself and the monster.

White and blue sparks jumped into existence as the stone teeth of the beast bit against the unbreakable steel of the artillery sword. The monster tried to exert its enormous strength by shattering the blade with its jaws, just as it was crushing the trachea of the mortal beneath it. The gladius, however, burning with the combined will of all mankind, won the struggle. Cutting through the flint teeth, the blade sliced the troll's head off just above its lower jaw.

The final creature ignored the old man, who was still gasping for air on the cold ground. It ran past the fallen warrior, and toward the warm lands just out of reach. Greedily sucking oxygen, he struggled to push the heavy corpse of his last kill off of his body. The old man would not let the last of the beasts reach his home. With all that was left within him, the old man flung the dead monster off of himself and pivoted backward into a kneeling position. The strangulation from moments before had left his vision blurred with dark spots. Nonetheless, he pulled the gladius over his shoulder and flung it with all the strength he could muster. It flew forward, tumbling end over end for the course of three revolutions before the blade pierced through what passed for the monster's heart.

The old man laughed as he watched the final invader fall. He had not known if the blade would find its mark, and watching it do so brought a joy into his heart that bordered on madness.

The joy was short lived. As the inky spots that had blurred his vision began to fade, the old man saw the most horrifying image he had ever laid eyes upon. From each shattered troll a hundred tiny, crystalline goblins had formed. Like a swarm of nightmarish faeries they descended upon his home, ushering the fimblewinter in behind them.

His wife and child now stood in the doorway of their home, afraid and confused. The old man screamed some incomprehensible epithet of rage and despair. Still with no limit on the fight within him, he tried to run toward the house and somehow save them.

As soon as he broke forward something grabbed at his legs, pulling him down into the icy ground. Trying to pull free, he looked at what had clutched onto him and saw that his fallen brothers of the confederacy, dead but moving, were dragging him down below the icy surface of the battlefield. He fought with all his strength, but he may as well have been a child wrestling a bear.

"It's over, Johnny, and there ain't no marching home," one of them hissed from a mouth that was missing the bottom jaw.

More undead hands grabbed at him, pulling him through the ice and waist-deep into the frigid ichor of the diseased soil. He turned his head once more to his family and home. The green grass was replaced with white frost and the house was cracking and screaming. His wife had fallen to the ground, a frozen, shriveled mummy. The worst sight, though, was the image of an army of tiny Devourers swarming upon his boy and eating their way into his flesh as he screamed for his father.

The old man tried to scream back for his boy, but the diseased blood of the earth filled his mouth and nose with the essence of pestilence. His final words came out as gurgled cries as his countrymen dragged him into oblivion.

CHAPTER SIX

Emmett breached the frozen surface of the slushy, ice-choked water and gasped for breath. The intensity of the cold in the air burned his lungs like fire. Better to breathe and burn than to not breathe at all, though.

Coughing and choking, he puked up water that tasted clean and fresh. Somewhere in the back of his mind this felt wrong. It should have been salt water, shouldn't it?

The river was massive, but slow-moving. The icy slush did not just sit upon its surface, but made up the entirety of the river, at least as far down as Emmett could feel. At any moment, Emmett feared, the whole body of water might stop flowing altogether and freeze into solid ice.

Emmett first looked to his left. He couldn't quite determine where the flow of slush ended and the snow-covered riverbank began, but a hundred yards or so away he could make out the image of a dwarfish creature with black, frostbitten skin and a long beard, the color of the winter sky before a snowfall. Braided into the creature's beard were shimmering bits of wealth, gold and silver and small stones of various shades. It wore a cloak of white fur and a hood made from the skinned head of a wolf. Beneath the cloak Emmett could see the shimmer of gold and silver necklaces, many of them, hanging about the dwarf's neck.

The short, broad-shouldered creature beckoned Emmett, curling its stubby index finger back and forth toward him. The summoning finger bore a three-piece ring that was jointed at each knuckle and glimmered with a solar radiance.

The dwarf put a mighty fear into Emmett's heart. It was not the strange proportions of the beckoning creature's body, nor its black, necrotized skin. It was the impatient manner in its stance and the greedy smile beneath its beard. There was an aura of insatiable hunger that emanated out from the creature. No, hunger was the wrong word. Greed. That was more accurate. It didn't need anything from Emmett. It desired something though, and with an intense, dangerous passion.

Emmett, still fighting to keep afloat in the river of slush, turned his gaze to the other embankment. The river's edge seemed as if it were probably a further swim on this side, and what Emmett saw may have stricken most men as a more dire situation than a single, suspicious dwarf.

Far off in the distance stood a massive tree, whose girth was wider than Emmett's field of vision, and whose heights reached above the misty, snow-driven sky. In front of this tree a bloody and vicious battle was taking place. Men with missing limbs, dressed in blood-soaked uniforms of Union blue, fought against Confederate soldiers with holes in their chests and pieces of skull missing. Among them was the odd Indian brave, riddled with rifle fire or belly cut open and leaking guts, pitting his anger against gray and blue alike. Their numbers were incalculable, as if the whole of each army were meeting on this final field to settle the war of the states once and for all.

For Emmett, in the horror to his right there was also hope.

Without looking back at the short creature on the other bank, Emmett began to swim toward land with a sense of urgency. If this was truly the whole of each American army, then his father would be there. His father would be there, a head above all the others, like Ajax at the sacking of Troy. His father would be there with answers, and action, and a way to fix everything. If Emmett could just swim to land, if he could see through the snow, and mist, and the smoke of rifle fire, and the spray of blood, then he would find salvation in the brilliant eyes and strong hands of the man who had given him life.

Emmett paddled and kicked as hard as his strong, young body could manage. The more he fought to reach land, the stronger the grip of the sucking slush became. After a few attempts to swim with all his gusto, and a few times nearly being sucked down below the freezing river, Emmett caught on to how things worked. He steeled himself to the burning cold, and forced his firework nerves to slow down.

Once he got control of body and mind, the boy let his body float on the surface and used his long arms to take slow, deep strokes that allowed him to glide through the slush. The going was slow, and the frigid slush sapped his strength and his will. There was no choice though. Emmett kept paddling.

When his hand finally hit solid ground, mid-stroke, it was visually indistinguishable from the slush river that he was submerged in. His sense of touch told a different story. What his hand found purchase against was solid ice, hard as bedrock and cold as death. Emmett pressed both hands against the frozen ground and pushed his aching, tired body up and away from the river's grasp. Somehow it was colder in the open air than it had been in the slush. Emmett was okay with this. He preferred the increased chill to the heavy death grip of the quagmire that he just escaped.

The battle raged around him, dead men hacking one another to pieces, yet still fighting. Cannons fired, leaving smoke that was indistinguishable from the steam rising out of their bodies—indistinguishable from the falling snow. No roaring powder blast accompanied the artillery's deadly payload. No cries, neither of death nor war, echoed from the gaping mouths of the angry and agonized. Swords clashed with no volume and horses screamed in silent protest. The realm of the auditory belonged to howling winds and creaking ice alone.

Emmett walked across the field in an almost somnambulant fashion. Slugs sped passed his head. Artillery shells exploded, raining shrapnel only yards away. Oblivious to the silent savagery around him, Emmett walked as if he were a ghost on an earthly battlefield.

Looking first left, then right, not slowing his pace, Emmett scanned the battlefield for his father. The warriors—gray, blue, and red alike—all stumbled, stepped, or rushed out of his path in an eerily coincidental-looking manner that, of course, was anything but. The scene was a sea of eternally dying soldiers, holding in their own intestines as they thrust bayonets, gray matter leaking from their empty eye sockets while they managed to still aim their rifles. Nowhere in Emmett's field of vision (which seemed much wider than it had any right to be) could he see the golden-haired giant who had provided the base material for his own over-sized body. All at once he came to understand why his father was not here in this icy hell. That understanding was accompanied by a great fear, casting a shadow over the simultaneous feelings of relief.

His father was, unsurprisingly, alive. The man was as strong, smart, and fearless as the Nordic gods he had told Emmett about as a child. Men like his father did not die in war. They won wars and sent others to their deaths. Emmett momentarily pondered how many of the condemned around him had been sent here by his pa.

A species of pride, the kind of codependent pride that parents and children mutually share for the other's accomplishments, burned in Emmett's heart. Even so, those warm feelings could not burn away the hopelessness that was descending upon him. If his father was not here, in these dead-lands, then what hope did Emmett have of escaping and returning to his sick mother?

As hope vanished from his heart, something far across the battlefield caught Emmett's eye. In the gnarled, rooted base of the massive tree that lay beyond the never-ending melee, there was something that looked like a throne carved into the tree. No, it wasn't carved. The twisting bases of the roots formed this gorgeous seat naturally. At least as naturally as anything may happen in this place.

Upon the root throne sat a woman, skin as pale as the falling snow. Her exposed flesh stood in stark contrast to the dark bark of the tree throne. Half of her was concealed in a shadow thrown by the contours of the tree. She was beautiful, easily the most beautiful woman Emmett had ever laid eyes upon. There was something terrible and cold in that beauty. It was the same kind of beauty that one might find in an ivory monolith that served the sole purpose of reminding humanity how ugly and small they are.

Awe and terror sent shivers through Emmett's body, far more powerful than anything the cold could evoke from him. Despite his fear, Emmett walked forward, through the freezing blood, the fallen bodies, and the crossfire of ethereal artillery. If the father whom he worshiped like a god could offer no help, then Emmett would throw himself at the feet of this realm's queen. He was sure that's what the enthroned woman with the alabaster skin was—the queen of the underworld, the goddess of death.

Emmett continued to walk forward, toward the throne of knotted wood. His eyes were locked upon the curves of the queen's strong, shapely body and the perfect features of her cold and uncaring face. He thanked whatever gods might be that shadows covered half of her, or else the entirety of her divine beauty might have driven him mad.

After what may have been days, Emmett finally made it across the killing field, and within yards of the Queen. In a sloppy, tired manner, Emmett allowed his knees to give out. He fell hard against the icy ground, into a kneeling position at the feet of death herself.

At this range he could now see that her right side was not simply concealed by shadows, but was shadow itself. Right down the middle was the goddess split. On the left was smooth skin of pure white, like ice-covered snow. Her right side was blacker than an abandoned mineshaft, and looked to have an insubstantial quality to it. Emmett imagined that her touch, from either the black hand or the white, would freeze the blood solid in his veins.

"State your business."

The goddess spoke without looking at Emmett. Her gaze was focused past him, toward the endless melee of the eternally dying. Emmett was grateful for this. Eyes are the windows to the soul, he thought, and intuition warned that staring into the vast soul of such a creature would do nothing good.

"I ..." Emmett faltered. The awe and fear he felt left his tongue feeling fat and numb in his mouth.

After a moment of silence the woman, who was death, repeated her command. There was no anger or annoyance in her voice. Just a cold, distant patience.

"State your business."

"I ..." Emmett gulped, but recovered his voice quickly this time. "I come to beg mercy. Mercy for my ma."

"Your mother will have my mercy soon, Emmett Wongraven."

Tears sprang up in Emmett's eyes. They streamed down and froze onto his cheeks.

"No. I want her to live. I'm asking you not to take my Ma away!"

"And what sacrifice do you offer with such a prayer, man-child?"

"Sacrifice?" The word seemed to hang in the air, and all at once Emmett thought he now understood why his prayers to the Christian god had gone unheard. He'd offered nothing in return.

"Hel must be made whole. Blood for blood and life for life."

"You mean ... you mean you'll save my mom if I give you something else?"

"Someone else."

This time the queen of the underworld set her eyes on Emmett's so that there might be no misunderstanding.

"Blood for blood," she spoke. "Life for life."

Emmett nodded in agreement. Her gaze, which bore upon him with the weight of a collapsing star, had robbed him of speech for the moment. When he could finally find the words, he spoke aloud.

"Blood for blood. Life for life."

CHAPTER SEVEN

The familiar smell of burning wood and boiling water poked and prodded at the old man's consciousness. As much as his mind and muscles wanted to stay asleep despite his nightmares, his stomach was screaming.

It smells like food, you great oaf! Get off your lazy ass!

This argument was hard to counter, and the old man found himself stirring into the waking world. While the smell of fire had awakened his hunger, he noticed even before opening his eyes that the air around him was warm and he had somehow found solace from the cold mountain winter.

There was a heaviness to his eyelids, but the old man exorcised his weariness and looked upon his surroundings. The hopes that his luck had changed with the temperature were short-lived. Inches above where he lay was a slab of solid rock. Below him he could feel hard-packed earth. To either side were only inches of space between the old man and walls of more solid rock. The old man craned his neck to find that the space in front of his head was sealed off by rusted iron bars. Beyond his confines, the old man could see the inside of a log cabin, illuminated by a dancing flame somewhere outside his field of vision. The place was Spartan. No furniture from what he could see. The only decoration was a crucifix above the door.

The course of events was unclear, but somehow he had exchanged the icy prison of snow for an earthen cage. Despite all odds, it seemed as if his situation may have actually worsened.

In search of his revolver, his hand pressed up against his side, only to find his bare skin. Unsurprisingly, his gun-belt and his weapons had been confiscated, but also his clothes. Whoever or whatever had captured him had left him as naked as the day he'd entered the world.

Some men may have panicked here, or called out, or wept. The old man was too measured in temperament for that. Instead he lay quietly, taking in the sounds, scents, and images around him. Through the bars near his head the old man could see shadows dancing on a nearby log wall. Judging from what he could make out of the cabin's structure, the old man guessed that he was still in the Sierra Nevada. The smell of food cooking and wood burning told him that his captor was not far off.

Several small sounds competed for prominence. A bubbling call said that water was coming to a boil somewhere close. A faint sniffling sound came from the same direction as the boiling— someone with a cold. A howling sound outside bespoke either great wind or angry angels nearby. Perhaps both.

One sound was louder than all the others. A whimpering moan, overflowing with grief and fear, reverberated from the outside of the cage and through the stone to the old man's right. It was impossible to distinguish whether the sound came from a man or an animal. Whatever it was seemed to be imprisoned in another stone box very close by.

Sounds of food gently splashing into water and the rattle of a wooden spoon stirring against a metal pot told the old man that whoever lived here was distracted enough that he may try his luck with the bars. Being a bull of a man, he found that his broad shoulders, thick chest, and impressive height filled the space of the horizontal prison in a rather tight way. To maneuver his arms over his head in the tight quarters took nearly fifteen minutes and a whole lot of discomfort.

Finally the old man got his calloused bear paws on the rusted bars. He could see where each went into a chiseled hole above them, and even saw phantoms of light through the space around where the iron met stone.

Slowly, but with a great, controlled force, the old man pushed up on the bars. To his pleasure, there was a little give. The bars raised, all in unison, about a quarter inch before catching on to something that locked them in place above. The bars and that which sealed them shut made a slight *ting* sound. It was faint, but evidently enough to distract his "host" from his cooking. The whimpering thing also temporarily stopped its crying.

All was silence for a moment. Soft plodding footsteps, like bare feet on a dirt floor, came the old man's way. A sniffle followed by a wet throat-clearing cough accompanied the foot falls. The person stopped just short of the old man's tiny cell.

"That you messing with your cage, pup?" a voice called out with a deep, hillbilly accent.

The voice was answered with only a louder, more emotional weeping.

"Don't fret none. I ain't ready for you today. You even get some dinner tonight. Gotta keep you alive and well for a few more days at least."

The old man was disturbed by the lack of malice in the hillbilly's voice. There seemed to be no hatred there, just a man telling it like it is.

The creature in the next cell began to cry hysterically now, and this time it was a distinctly human sobbing.

The captor walked a few more steps, stopping by where the old man was imprisoned. Once again he began to speak in that matter of fact tone.

"Or did you finally wake up, you big sonofagun?"

The old man didn't stir or make a noise, save for slow, even breaths. The thought that he might still be asleep was the only advantage he had right now. While it was unclear just why this man had pulled him out of a snowy grave just to imprison him elsewhere, the old man guessed that it wouldn't be for anything pleasant.

The mountain man bent down next to the bars. His hot, putrid breath beat against the old man's head as he spoke.

"You's awake, all right. Manage to wriggle those tree trunk arms up over yer head too."

With the celerity of a rattlesnake, the old man's left hand struck out through the bars, ready to snatch his new enemy by the face or throat. The spacing of the bars was narrow though, and the old man's forearm got caught between the bars just shy of the mountain man.

The rusted bars bit into his skin, making him wince. Laughter and a howl of surprised relief came from the hillbilly's mouth.

"Wooo-eeee, you be quick as you are big!" the old man's captor said with a chuckle. "A bit too big for squeezing through them bars though, hoss."

Unable to grasp his enemy, the old man withdrew his arm. Half sticking out, it was vulnerable to the whims of the man outside.

"The Lord, he sure do deliver! A week or so in there'll tender up those gamey muscles. After that you'll make vittles for a fortnight."

The man outside the cage stood up and began walking away. He continued addressing the old man.

"Found you in the nick o' time too. These scrawny-ass other folk I got will be lucky to last me another two weeks, and it ain't like there's much eating out there this time of year."

A sloshing liquid mixed with the nearby whimpering of the person who was presumably caged up just like the old man. Footsteps back in his direction followed. They stopped by the bars above his head once more.

"You're lucky though. Tonight you get to eat. Maybe you'll appreciate it, unlike the little shit next door here. Gotta keep that meat good for the next few weeks, right?"

Something damp and hot came flying through the bars and landed on the old man's chest. After a moment he realized it was a hunk of meat. He supposed that it wasn't beef or wild game.

"Don't get all persnickety, now. That's a good hunka meat, and I know you must be hungry."

While his mind reeled with disgust, the smell of cooked meat made the old man's stomach growl and his mouth water. He wasn't sure how long he'd been unconscious, but it felt as though food was distant memory. More important than his gnawing hunger was his need for strength. Hunger would dull him, and if he died here, dinner to some desperate hillbilly, then his son would be doomed. For his son's life, the old man was more than willing to sacrifice one of the last bits of his innocence and engage in this heinous act.

Without any show of emotion, the old man began to devour the hunk of human meat. Years of war and decades of living in the West had made a survivor out of the old man. A big part of outliving your competition was staying observant and alert. So the old man drove the anger and frustration from his mind, focusing on his surroundings, hoping to unearth some factor he could leverage.

The thing whimpering in the cage next to him, he was fairly certain, was a child. The food cooking not too far off was probably the meat from one of the kid's parents. They must have been heading west, trying to beat the winter. It seemed more than a little lucky for this hungry madman that he had found the unconscious, snow entombed body of the old man amongst the vast Sierra Nevada. But as the cannibal had said, *The Lord, he sure do deliver.*

A chair dragged against the dirt floor and the hillbilly sat down with a sloshing bowl of man-stew. Soft and solemn utterances escaped his lips, thanking God for his bounty. After saying grace, the cannibal slurped down his food with all the grace of rabid dog. Once dinner was done, the old man heard him walk to a deeper part of the house. The sound of footfalls ceased and was followed by a long yawn and the soft crunch of hay under a reclining body.

The light from some flame still danced on the wall that the old man could see, but there were no sounds save for the occasional wood pop, and an inconsistent whimpering. Eventually a soft snoring joined the gentle chorus.

Lying quiet, trapped between earth and iron, the old man took stock of his prison. Solid stone met him on the sides and up above. Hard packed dirt made up the floor. Even if he could maneuver himself to start digging at the floor, he wouldn't be able to tunnel out without his captor noticing.

His mind wandered to the tunnels that the Chinese workers blew through the mountains, bit by bit. How would one of the rail workers get out of this situation, if trapped? They would probably die, he reckoned. Then the old man eyed the space above his, where the bars went through the stone, and he found his answer. He would need time, and more than a little cleverness in gathering the necessary tools. For now he planned to test the worth of the tool closest at hand—the whimpering child in the cell beside him.

"Hey, it's gonna be okay," the old man said in a coarse but reassuring whisper. The whimpering continued.

"I know you're scared. This is scary. We can get out of this mess if we work together though." His whisper was a bit louder now, but still low enough as to not to stir their sleeping captor.

The crying slowed down to a barely controlled sniffling. The boy gave no answer yet, but he was calming down. That was a step in the right direction, and the old man could be patient, when patience was called for. He allowed the boy another few moments.

"What's your name?"

"Hank," the boy replied after a few more seconds of sniffling.

"Well listen, Hank. I need you to do me a favor. I need you to quietly tell me everything you've seen and heard. I'm guessing it'll be painful to recollect, but any chance we have at surviving lies in what you can tell me."

"He ... the motherfucker killed my pa." The words were angry and louder than the old man had hoped for. The cannibal's snoring paused for a moment, making the old man fear that the game was over. A few seconds passed and the snoring returned with a fierceness, snorting at the apnea like an angry pig.

The boy was weeping again, no doubt at the thought of his father being butchered and cooked only feet from where he now lay.

"I know it hurts, Hank. It burns like hell. But we gotta stay smart and quiet. I'm a father myself, and I can tell you, the greatest honor you can do your parents is surviving this. Can you do that, Hank? Can you help make sure we both survive this?"

Still crying, Hank's quivering voice replied simply, "Yes."

"Okay. Now tell me everything. How you and your pa got here. Everything you've seen, heard, or smelled. Any of it could be our ticket to getting out of here."

"That ain't enough. He's evil and I want him dead. You promise me we'll kill him."

The old man could hear that the hatred and anger in the boy's voice were white-hot, and not likely to cool with time. It saddened him to hear that kind of venom from such a small voice, but he also understood that the need was real. If the boy didn't see his father's killer dead, then the anger would poison him for life. If he was allowed to cut the bastard down he may be haunted by the weight of murder for the rest of his life, but such a burden was easier carried than the disease of hate-fueled madness.

"Don't you worry, little man. I'm something of an old hand when it comes to putting down evil things."

***

Hank had told the old man everything he could remember. How his family was crossing the mountains to start a new life in California, now that they were free. How his mother had taken ill and passed away, slowing up their trek into the mountains. How the winter had come early this year, making travel deadly and slow.

The cold had almost killed them more than once, but turning back would have been just as dangerous as trudging forward at that point. Then one night, after waiting out a blizzard in a cave, the boy and his father had eyed the white, controlled smoke of a fireplace or a stove. They reckoned it must be a house, or at least a camp of some sort. Although the father had been unsure what kind of hospitality they might receive at its source, it had to be better than dying of exposure. It turned out he was wrong.

What they found was a finely crafted cabin, oddly out of place this deep in the mountains. Its log form was mostly of a typical construction, aside from how it seemed to merge right into the rock of an adjacent cliff face. Smoke had still been pouring out of the chimney when they arrived, and Hank remembered how he could almost feel the warmth inside.

Hank's father had knocked on the door, and was more than a little surprised by how warmly he was greeted by this stranger. The cabin's owner had invited them in and offered each a plate of hot, bitter stew made from roots and some manner of vegetable paste. There had been something else in the stew too—something that made sleep come upon them with the same gentle quickness as the heat that warmed their bones and their bellies.

In hindsight, Hank told the old man, he could see there was something wrong with situation. Their host was strangely elated upon seeing two weary travelers show up at his doorstep. And after he served dinner, the mountain man had said grace and thanked god for his bounty, not their bounty, just his. And he hadn't even been eating alongside them.

Hank went on to tell how he hadn't even made it through his meal before he passed out. When he came to, he was locked in what he called a stone coffin, with iron bars set by his head. His forced slumber had saved him from seeing his father's actual death. But when he awoke, he heard the sounds of the mountain man's cleaver butchering the man who had raised him. Hank, being a child, had found the room to maneuver himself so that he could look back through the bars. What he saw was the severed head of his pa. A lifeless, grown version of his own face, discarded to the dirt floor like so much offal. Hank had been strong up until this point, but now he began to sob once more. With a trembling voice he recounted how he had been unable to close his eyes or turn away as the hillbilly unceremoniously cut his father apart as easily as one might dress a buck.

Hank broke down into quiet sobbing as he relived the terrible moments. The old man had planned on giving him a few minutes before pushing him more. Hank started talking first, though, and his words confirmed what the old man already suspected.

"And you ain't gonna believe me 'bout what happened next, but it's the truth," Hank said with a quiver in his voice.

"I've grown a pretty high tolerance for the unbelievable, Hank."

"He took the bowl that he used to catch my dad's blood, and walked to the door over there. He climbed up on a stump of wood so he could reach the crucifix hung up over the doorway, and poured my dad's blood over the cross."

Hank's words were distant as he told this part, as if the events were too surreal for his mind to fathom.

"He said some kind of prayer as he poured it over the cross. Something about blood for blood and flesh for flesh. I was already so afraid, but then ..."

"Then what?" the old man asked, barely above a whisper.

"Jesus talked back to him. Not just in voice, neither. I could see his mouth moving from across the room. His wooden body squirming on the cross, like he was a living thing. He told him a stranger was coming. I'm guessing that's you. Said you were an animal sick with grief and that killing you would be a mercy."

The old man smiled in his cramped, prison of stone, earth and iron. A faint laugh even escaped his lips.

"Are you ... laughing?" Hank asked with amazement and a bit of fear.

"He's getting scared," the old man said, more to himself than in reply to Hank. "Means I'm getting close."

Hank wondered what the old man was talking about, but there was something in his brief laughter that was unsettling. Neither of them spoke for the rest of the night, and the old man settled into a restful sleep, trapped in the den of the cannibal witch.

CHAPTER EIGHT

Golden sunlight poured down from the powder blue sky, reflecting off of the sepia earth and casting a healthy glow across the green leaves of the endless orange trees. The intensity of the day's brightness assaulted Emmett's eyes and head, causing the young man an ache that dominated his frontal lobe.

"I ain't paying you to nurse no hangover, redskin," Harvey Mackum said in a nasal admonishment.

Emmett shook off the pain in his head and tossed a large sack of oranges into Mackum's cart. It was the fifth sack of oranges he'd picked that afternoon, which brought him up to twenty-five cents for the day so far.

"That's the problem with you Injun-blooded bastards. One or two shots of rye and you're aching for a week," Mackum said, believing himself helpful. "Gotta build some tolerance if you're gonna make it in the white man's world."

"Wasn't drinking," Emmett replied with little interest or emotion as he grabbed an empty sack that was hanging from a nail on the back of the cart.

Under normal circumstances, Emmett had little patience for Harvey Mackum's breed of instructional bigotry. Today his mind was far too preoccupied with where the last week had disappeared to take offense or to note Mackum's words.

This morning Emmett had awoken in his own bed. The sunlight stabbed between the shutters of his bedroom window, prodding him awake like golden daggers. How he had gotten home, he had no clue. Nor could he think quite clearly about any subject, to be truthful. His head and eyes ached with sharp, throbbing malignancy. Every muscle in his body felt as if it had been marinated in pain.

According to his mother and Mary Coughlin, no one had heard him come home. They had simply found him in his bed yesterday morning, burning up with fever. Six days had passed between when he had entered the *Cavern of The First Breath* and today. Aside from incredibly vivid and disturbing fever dreams, Emmett could account for none of this time.

To throw more coal onto the fire, his extended disappearance had set his mother into such worry that her condition had now worsened. Her cough was no more violent, but the fits came with increasing frequency. Her nearly nonexistent appetite had shriveled into nothingness. Her sunken face and frail body looked already dead, rather than dying.

In short, time was running out, and Emmett had burned up a good bit of it.

Mary Coughlin had been good enough to stay with his mother for the extra days. She was a fine and kind old lady if there had ever been one. She was in no position to work for free though, and Emmett had to spend almost all of his remaining funds to compensate her for her time. As such, he had to head out this day, with his pounding head and confused state of mind, to rustle up some quick cash. This is how he ended up five miles away on Mackum's fourteen-acre orange grove. It was time for harvest, and he knew the man always paid, even if he was something of a prick.

Mackum stepped up next to Emmett and grabbed a burlap sack for himself. The man was small in stature and abrasive in personality, and had all the good looks of a stillborn weasel, but he was hardworking and honest. There were plenty of charismatic, lazy men who would smoke cigars while others sweated for them. Mackum wasn't one of those. He worked alongside his men and set the pace, all the while paying a mite fairer wage than those other types of employers. These traits made the Irish-blooded farmer respectable, if not likable.

"Word around town was you up and vanished for more'n a week. I figured you followed your pa into that damn-fool war."

Mackum's voice sounded muffled and distant, the mocking voice of a murderer to a man being drowned.

Emmett grabbed an orange the size of a grapefruit. His eyes were transfixed on the spot where two branches met upon the trunk of the orange tree. Above the knot where the two branches became one was a hollow that held an uncanny resemblance to the living throne of wood where death had been seated in his dream. For the better part of a minute Emmett stared at this image that had escaped his mind and shifted into the real world. It was different, of course, smaller and vacant. Instead of being half-buried in darkness and obscured by sheets of snow, this hollow was canopied by leaves that offered only a soft shadow of concealment. Still, Emmett felt with all his heart that he was looking at the seat of Hell's queen.

"Emmett? You deaf, boy?" Mackum yelled, stirring Emmett from his reverie.

Emmett turned and looked at him blankly, trying to cope with the idea that death had followed him.

"If you ain't here up there," Mackum said while reaching up and poking the much taller teenager in the forehead, "then I don't need you here at all".

Emmett realized now that Mackum had been talking to him the whole time, no doubt in some demeaning manner. The man was angry now. He didn't take well to being ignored on his own land by folks he was paying.

"Sorry. I'm just kind of ..." Emmett began, trying to banish the images from his dream, which were now returning with titanic force. "My ma's getting worse. It's hard to focus on anything else."

"Well, you got my condolences, kid. If you ain't fit to work though, you need to get to stepping. If you ain't making me money, then you ain't making money, neither. Can't have some big, moping oaf slowing down my pace."

Emmett wanted to hate the farmer for his callousness, but he couldn't. There was something in his honesty that appealed to Emmett. It reminded him of his father in a way. While Emmett's pa might show more tact, he was never one to beat around the bush or distort the truth.

There were other things about Mackum that reminded Emmett of his father. He was hardworking and full of life. The farmer might not have been a handsome, broad-chested giant like his pa, but he had that same limitless energy and iron will.

"Sorry, Mr. Mackum. I'll speed it up. We need the money"

And Emmett did pick up the pace. He picked oranges just as fast as Mackum, but stayed at trees longer, as his height allowed him to grab more fruit. The farmer, always a tree or two ahead, kept yapping in his ugly, nasal voice. He voiced his dislike for the Confederate troublemakers, as well as the nigger-loving Yankees for bringing war to the continent. He bragged about his fruit and his trees, challenging Emmett to name one farm he'd ever seen with finer oranges. He bitched about the how the Jew lawman in town had failed to track down the bastards who kept stealing his alpacas in the night.

All of this was just background noise to Emmett. Consumed by his own thoughts—thoughts of spiteful grandfathers, and hidden caves, and dying mothers—Emmett only turned his full attention toward Mackum when he ended a sentence with the words "blood for blood".

"What was that?" Emmett asked, shooting a glance of such urgency and fear in Mackum's direction that the farmer actually stumbled backward.

"Blood for blood," Mackum replied, eyeing Emmett nervously. "Saying if that Christ-killer, Silver, was worth the copper in his badge, then I'd see some justice. And not some New York City, dandy justice. I mean blood for blood."

Two thoughts occurred to Emmett just after Mackum stopped speaking. The first was that his words were a sign. The queen of death would take Mackum in trade. Mackum, with his wiry muscles and strong hands. Mackum, whose limitless energy nurtured life across fourteen acres. Mackum, who treated him like so much redskin garbage. Yes, death would trade his mother for the man before him.

His second thought, which flashed into his mind almost simultaneously, was how foolish and mad his father would think him right now. To even consider sacrificing a living, breathing man, on the word of a nightmare and some stone-age mysticism, was paramount to insanity. Such deadly madness, his father had said more than once, was where all superstition eventually led. Abraham slaying his son, Aztecs killing so that the sun may rise, Arabs and Christians murdering one another for the claim of desert ruins— faith, wherever it may be placed, always led to doom.

This act, if he chose to go through with it, would not be murder for some allegorical deity or a lifeless idol. Slaying Mackum, here in this field of green and orange, would not be a sacrifice to the titanic goddess of death. It would be a sacrifice to the living goddess of his birth so that she might live, and a sacrifice to his father, so that he might come home to the woman he loved. This would not be an act of superstition. It would be a business transaction, between Emmett and some force that lay just beyond the grip of understanding.

Blood for blood—Mackum's words were but one sign that day. Another spoke in a stronger, if more subtle voice. This was the fact that no one else had shown up at the farm looking for work this morning. On a beautiful day, where a man pays a fair wage, such lack of interest was downright unnatural. There was Elijah Hewitt, of course, Mackum's full-time hand, but he was working acres away. More importantly, Emmett's late rising had brought him to the farm hours after sunrise. Elijah had already been hard at work by then, leaving no one but Mackum to know that Emmett had even been here.

As many as thirty oranges were in Emmett's sack right then. He flexed his arm up and down, taking measure of the weight in the bag. It was heavy, but Emmett was strong. The young man felt confident he could swing the sack with enough force to knock Mackum off of his feet. Mackum was a tough little bastard. A hit like that wouldn't knock him out, but it'd stun him. Emmett reckoned that would be enough.

Using his thumbnail, which had grown a bit too long and far too dirty since his trek to the Paiute reservation, Emmett cut into the skin of an orange that had yet to make it into his sack. With a quick motion he peeled off a big hunk of the rind, and then another, exposing a good portion of the sweet, wet fruit within. Mackum was still yapping up ahead, with his back turned to Emmett. He hadn't noticed a thing. If he had, he'd be screaming his head off at Emmett for stealing his produce.

Emmett closed in on Mackum. The sack of oranges was slung over his shoulder and he held it one hand. The half-peeled fruit was in the other. With a pivot of his hips Emmett swung the bag out to the side, with all the force of an overturned trebuchet. The sack caught Mackum in the left shoulder and the side of the head. The unsuspecting farmer spun for a quarter rotation before hitting the dirt hard. His mouth and nose collided with the knotted roots of a nearby orange tree, and both burst open with blood.

Mackum rolled over, stunned but furious, just in time to see the massive sixteen-year-old fall down upon him. Emmett's knees landed on Mackum's shoulders with all the grace and care of a drunken buffalo. The boy bore down on the farmer's chest, pushing the air from his lungs.

"Mother fucker!" Mackum began to scream, spraying spit and blood from his mouth. He only managed the "Mother fu—" before Emmett's right hand smashed the half-peeled orange into his mouth, like a comically large gag.

Emmett could feel Mackum twisting and writhing against his weight. He could hear the mumbled, muffled screams against the sweet, pulpy gag. None of this would do the man any good. Emmett had him now, and he had gone too far to turn back. Mackum would be delivered to the dual-toned death goddess of his dream. A trade for his mother's life.

Tipping the sack upside down, Emmett let the thirty or so oranges tumble into the rich California dirt. With the sack empty, Emmett pulled it over the farmer's head, hiding his panicked, hateful gaze. Once the burlap was pulled over Mackum's face, Emmett wrapped his big, meaty hands, hands far too big for a kid his age, around the farmer's throat.

He thanked whatever gods may be for the sack. Somehow he doubted that he could have looked Mackum in the eye while he killed him. The sickening sensation of a trachea collapsing beneath his fingers was bad enough (for some reason Emmett thought that crushing a sparrow in his fist would feel much the same). To look into a familiar face, or any face for that matter, while committing such a gruesome and despicable act would have been too much for Emmett to bear, even in his mother's name.

But the burlap sack was there, just as the other workers were not. Through the coarse material, Emmett could see no terror, pain, or yearning. There was only the rough-hewn, brown landscape of the sack, approximately the same shape as a man's face. Someone or something was watching out for him, Emmett thought, supplying him the tools to save his ma. Giving him the means to be a hero.

CHAPTER NINE

The unmistakable sound of a gunshot stirred the old man awake. Another shot followed, and the old man could tell that the blast hadn't come from a hunting rifle. It was the crack of a .44 caliber cartridge revolver—the war cry of his own pistol.

Pain earned from a slumber spent in the tiny confines of a cell that he barely fit into wracked the old man's muscles. Small rocks embedded within the hard-packed soil on which he lay dug into his back. His tongue and throat felt as dry as desert sand, as the fire burning within the cabin's stove had banished the humidity from the air. Between his teeth he could feel the bits of the human flesh that he was fed the night before, and the thought brought a wave of nausea over him. Still, there was a cautious optimism in his heart.

That optimism was his greatest weapon against the Devourers and their servants. The beasts from beyond the stars, as well as the witches who served them, fed off of base emotions like fear and despair.

The old man would not sustain his enemy, nor could he. Long ago he had bled out the last of such feelings. The old man was calm and cool on the outside, but no cold emotions or hollowness lay in his heart. Below his patient exterior, reflected in his steel-gray eyes, there was a furnace of white-hot love and hate. These twin forces consumed his entirety, leaving no room for Thurs and his lot to lay their hooks into him.

"You know how long he's been out there?" the old man asked, unsure if Hank was awake.

"Not long," Hank's voice echoed from his own stone cell. "Mumbled something about some crows he's feuding with."

Another two shots rang off in quick succession, cutting of Hank's words. The old man was keeping a mental tally, accounting for the rounds that the cannibal was wasting.

"I've counted four shots. Did you hear any more before I woke up?"

"No. He's only fired the four times."

Another two cracks fired, within seconds of each other. Unless he'd had the forethought to grab some extra ammo, he'd be coming back in soon.

"Sounds like he ain't faring so well against wise old Corvus."

"Who's Corvus?" Hank asked with a bit of confusion and refreshing childishness that the old man was surprised to find still present in the boy.

"It's Latin for crow." The old man left it at that, figuring the boy didn't need any schooling given their predicament. When Hank replied with an inquisitive "Oh?" he thought that maybe the boy could deal with something to distract him, and refined his explanation.

"Not really for crow. It refers to that whole family of blackbirds, all the different types of 'em."

The conversation was turning bittersweet for him. Memories of explaining and examining the difference between animals with his boy came flooding back to him. The old man had a passing knowledge of wildlife, partly from books, but mostly from traveling across the great stretches of North America. His wife, while unacquainted with Latin, had been able to tell the subtle differences between creatures with just a glance. Between the two of them, they had taught their son about naturalism and the wonders of the wild.

"Where'd you learn Latin? You go to priest school or something?"

The old man stifled a laugh. "No, nothing of that sort. Always liked to build stuff and tinker, so I went to university for a spell to study engineering. University folks are just as fond of dead languages as the Catholics are."

The door to the cabin burst open, ending the momentary illusion that the two were in a normal situation, chatting about mundane subjects. Cold air rushed in behind the cabin's owner, chilling the structure's entire volume.

The old man crossed his arms over his chest and got ready to make his move.

"Piece of shit gun," the hillbilly said as he slammed the door shut behind him.

"It's a poor tradesman that blames his tools," the old man replied, loud enough for the angry cannibal to hear him.

Hank gasped and in an audible whisper said, "What are you doing?"

"What the hell did you just say to me?" the mountain man growled back.

"Just saying, that's a fine pistol. Made it myself. Modeled after the Colt Dragoon, but designed for cartridges instead of ball and powder. Quick reload, and enough stopping power to put down a grizzly."

"Fire's for shit. You make lousy weapons."

"Ain't my fault you ain't got no aim." The old man spoke the words, staring at the stone ceiling of his cell, just inches from his face. The fact that he refused to crane his neck to look at his captor was a deliberate, subtle show of disrespect.

"That gun's a faithful weapon that just shoots where you tell it," he continued.

"Faithful to you, maybe. That what these lines carved into the barrel mean? They some kind o' curse, so's no one else can shoot it worth a damn?"

"No, ain't a curse. Those lines spell out its name. Tools of great quality deserve a name of their own."

"So what's it say?"

"Donner. It's the German word for Thunder. It has earned the name. Even god trembles when its iron is trained on him."

The mountain man approached the old man's cell with anger in his heart.

"I won't be having blasphemy like that in my home!"

The old man could hear Hank scurrying away from the bars in the cell next to him. Fear of the monster's rage may have filled the boy, but the old man had been banking on it.

"That's why he told you how to find me, you know? Because he's yeller. I'm not a free meal. I'm the killer on his tail."

The mountain man bent down, just out of the old man's reach, anger and confusion on his face.

"The boy told you that God talks to me! Don't pretend you knew that on your own!"

"You think you're the only one who's talked to god?" The old man let a manufactured laugh trail out after his words.

"You don't know nothing!" the cannibal screamed.

In a calm voice, still intentionally looking straight up into the stone above, the old man replied, "I know that the only thing keeping you alive right now ain't god, but the bars between us. Maybe you should start praying to them."

"You..." the cannibal's voice was quivering with emotion now. "You're the one who should be praying!"

The cannibal slammed the business end of the pistol, whose name he couldn't read, through the bars and into the top of the old man's head.

"How about I just blow—" That was as far as his question went before the old man's hand shot between the bars like a rattler.

Rawhide hands with the strength of a man who's worked hard his whole life gripped the hillbilly's wrist and pulled his arm, along with the revolver, back through the bars.

The old man had not made it through life in the west, the war of the states, and a crusade against the children of Utgard by underestimating anyone. Whatever else might be said about his captor, he was sure that a man who lived in such harsh conditions would be plenty strong. His enemy was off balance, surprised, and overwhelmed with anger, but this advantage would vanish soon. As quickly as he had pulled the hillbilly's arm into the cell, he leveraged the man's arm against the bars, simultaneously crushing his wrist within his vice-like grip.

After a few seconds of sudden and intense pain, the cannibal lost his grip and the revolver fell. The old man leveraged his enemy's arm against the bars harder, for a second longer, just to insure that he would instinctively pull his arm back instead of grabbing for the pistol. Suddenly the old man let him go and, sure enough, the hillbilly pulled his arm back with lightning quickness. He pulled away so fast, in fact, that the momentum caused him to fall on his ass.

"Motherfucker!" the hillbilly yelled, rubbing his arm where the old man had seemingly tried to break it off.

"I guess the bars ain't doing a great job of protecting you either," the old man said in a dry tone as he pulled the revolver down to his side. "Better pray harder."

"You just laugh it up in there! I was gonna do you quick and clean, keep you fed 'til your time was up. Now I'm just gonna let you die of thirst in there. Real ugly way to go, you'll see."

The cannibal got to his feet, angry and hurting.

"And you can keep your piece of shit gun. I used all the bullets. Lotta good it'll do you."

The old man traced the acid-etched runes on the barrel of his pistol with one finger. He hoped that setting off the bastard on the other side of the bars wouldn't endanger Hank. As much as that might sadden him though, the child's life would be an acceptable loss. The only thing that mattered was his own boy. If he had to leave a mountain of corpses behind him to save his son, so be it.

The rest of the day went by with a dreadful slowness, and nothing more of note happened. The old man stayed silent for the rest of the day. Hank kept quiet as well, aside from the occasional weeping. The mountain man went about his daily routine. Twice throughout the day he went outside to gather hunks of Hank's father that he had kept frozen in the snow outside and made an afternoon stew, followed by a dinner of meat he roasted on a stick over the flames of his stove. At each meal he prayed, perhaps a bit louder than usual, just for the old man to hear. Twice he came to Hank with water, making a show of it for the old man's benefit. Eventually he went to sleep, resting his body for the continuation of his spartan existence the next day.

Once the still of night arrived, and the unwitting servant of Thurs had been snoring for the better part of an hour, the old man got to work. Careful not to make any unnecessary noise, he brought the pistol up to his chest and released the secret compartment in the grip. A piece of walnut, notched perfectly to hold two .44 cartridges, pulled out from the gun. The emergency rounds gleamed in the dim, dancing firelight.

He reached his hand out between the bars and up, checking once more if he could locate whatever locked them in place. Whatever was keeping the cell locked was out of his reach. This left him with the less desirable option. The old man wasn't the type to drag out the unpleasant though.

Careful not to spill anything, he popped the cap off of the backside of the round, exposing the powder inside. He then emptied the powder from the first round into one hand, and began packing it in the space between one of the bars and the hole in the stone that it passed through. He did this with slow and careful precision to limit the loss of any powder. Once the space was packed full of gunpowder, he opened the second round and repeated the process with another bar, two places over.

That night the old man didn't sleep. He lay awake until morning, waiting for the cannibal to go outside and retrieve the ingredients for breakfast from his stash of human flesh. Once the door to the cabin closed behind him, the old man sprang into action.

"Hank, cover your ears. It's time," his voice came out drier and coarser than he had expected. Nearly two days without water had taken a toll on him.

"Time? You can get us out?"

The old man didn't reply. He knew that he had only moments to act before the cannibal hillbilly would return. He only hoped that his dehydrated, sore body would be able to drag itself out of this earthen prison quickly enough.

The old man covered his face with one arm, taking special care to protect his eyes, and scraped the iron on the edge of his gun against the stone above him, right where he had packed the gunpowder. After two hard drags across the stone a spark hit the powder, causing a loud bang. The old man felt tiny pieces of stone shrapnel rain down upon his naked flesh. The sulfurous smell of spent powder wafted into his nostrils, sparking a rush of adrenaline.

With a sense of urgency, he scraped the iron sight against the stone where he had packed his second charge. This time the spark caught the powder right away. Another loud pop was followed with more debris falling upon him. If the stone around the bars had been compromised enough by the blasts, he might be able to escape. If not, then he was surely a dead man.

For the first time since being locked away in the tiny space, the old man was glad that the cell was too small for him. Tucking his chin to his chest, he extended his scrunched up legs, pressing against the stone wall with his feet and driving his shoulders into the bars. His cramped, water-starved muscles protested and screamed. Even dehydrated, hungry, sore, and without rest, the old man's great size made him stronger than many men half his age. The stone around the bars began to give, signaling that the powder had done its work.

With one more push from his massive leg muscles, the old man pushed the iron bars clear through the crumbling stone. Just as he had freed his shoulders from the cell, extending his body fully for the first time in days, the mountain man came rushing back in through the door.

The sight of the old man crawling out from the smoking, broken cell froze the cannibal with shock. After a moment of initial disbelief, he ran across the room and pulled a hunting knife out from a wooden stump that lay near the bed of hay where he slept. He spun around to see the old man rising to his feet, naked and bleeding from small cuts and scrapes that littered his body. Until this moment, set against the backdrop of powder born smoke and life or death struggle, the mountain man had not truly realized how large his quarry was, nor just how scary the man could be.

The hillbilly raised his knife and took a wide stance, more practical for capturing an animal than for fighting another person. The old man, in turn, raised his revolver, tipping the barrel toward the sky, so that it bisected his face. With his right hand he made a dramatic, upward gesture, running his first two fingers across the inscription on the barrel. This movement was a bluff that held no arcane meaning, but he hoped it would distract the hillbilly from the fact that he had no ammo.

The hillbilly knew little of magic, despite unwittingly serving the Devourers. He bought the old man's bluff. What he did read correctly was the look in the old man's eyes, and that surrender would mean certain death. Rather than die on his knees, the cannibal lunged forward with his knife, risking whatever spell the naked beast of a man before him might cast.

The old man sidestepped and grabbed the cannibal by the wrist of his knife hand. Holding his enemy's arm up high, the old man swung to strike him in the face with the butt of his pistol.

Before he could follow through on this, the cannibal smashed his booted heel down onto the old man's bare foot. A tidal wave of pain shot through his foot and up his leg, and his grip on the cannibal lessened.

With a great tug that caused him to stumble back, the mountain man freed his hand and the weapon it held. He shuffled to the left, trying to get a better angle on the old man, who was still distracted by the pain in his foot.

Risking it all, the cannibal lunged, as he would onto a wounded animal. The old man sidestepped again, this time grabbing his captor by the hair and using his own momentum to send him falling forward, into the cast iron stove. A sickening thunk and sizzling sound followed the hillbilly's face smashing against the burning hot cast iron. If he had fallen down just inches to the right, his head would have gone right into the fire, where the door had long ago rusted off of its hinges.

The folly of instinct caused the man eater to push himself back, away from the thing that was burning his face, and in turn pressed his hands against the stove's surface. He screamed with pain as he fell away from the stove, leaving some of his flesh behind on the scalding surface.

The old man pressed his advantage. He pounced as the cannibal stumbled backward on his knees. With a quick movement he took hold of his enemy's hair from behind and slammed the barrel of his pistol into the base of his skull. The hillbilly slouched forward a little, but maintained his consciousness. Not wishing to let the man eater regain his senses, the old man ended the battle by shoving his captor into the open front of the stove, all the way to his shoulders.

The cannibal let out a hellish cry that chilled Hank's blood. His body twitched and convulsed, protesting the pain like an angry child. His hands pressed hard against the stove, willing to let themselves burn away if it meant saving the head. Despite his desperation, the hillbilly couldn't overpower the naked crusader's patient, iron hold.

After more seconds than it was pleasant to think about, the twitching and screaming stopped. The cannibal's body fell limp, allowing the flames to feast upon him in peace. The only sounds in the cabin were the crackle of burning tissue and burning wood, set against the old man's heavy breathing.

The old man released his grip on the dead hillbilly and eyed his own hand. He had had to hold it uncomfortably close to the fire in order to maintain the proper leverage on his captor. The heat had left its mark. Several angry, red blisters were already forming on the back of his hand. Without uttering a word the old man limped over toward the door of the cabin. He opened it and thrust his burned hand into the snow outside. It took the edge off.

Naked, hurt, and dehydrated, he reached up above the door and grabbed the effigy of Christ off of the wall. He looked at it with anger, wondering how many other myths and ideologies the Devourers hid behind. Then, almost as an afterthought, he tossed the crucifix into the fire, letting the idol burn along with its servant.

He spun around in a slow circle taking in the whole of the cabin for the first time. Looking at where he had been imprisoned, he could see there were three cells, including his own. A shelf of stone jutted out from the one wall of the cabin that was natural cliff face. Below it, three sections of stone had been hollowed out, either by man or nature. The cannibal, or whoever had built the place, had somehow cored holes through the top of the stone shelf and down into the hollows beneath. Five iron bars went through the cored holes above each hollow and were joined into a wooden slat that ran horizontally. The wooden slat was in turn held in place by a metal rod that slid across it and into another hole cored into the cliff face behind it. All three cells were like this, except of course the one that the old man had just destroyed.

He pulled away the iron rod that held Hank's bars in place and flung it back against the body of the man he had just killed. He then hunched over and pulled up the wooden slat and the attached bars, freeing Hank from the hole he had been trapped in.

The old man looked at the boy's dark skin and shaggy mess of hair as he inched toward freedom. Perhaps if it wasn't for Thurs and what had happened to his own boy, he might have found room for some bitterness toward the Negro boy. Plenty of his Confederate brothers had carried a deep hatred for colored folks, blaming the whole war on them. There was no room for further animosity in his heart though, especially for another human being. His ire was exclusively reserved for those dark things what lay beyond, and the witches that serve them.

The old man backed away, giving Hank space to come out. The boy did so slowly, like an animal expecting to be struck by the hand of a cruel master. He exited the cell and stood up for the first time in longer than he could account for.

The boy was a filthy wreck. His ribs jutted out, and his body was covered in scrapes. Smears of dirt and dried tears marred his face. Lack of quality rest had left the boy with bags under his eyes.

"You alright, boy? You can sit for a spell." Despite his pain and exhaustion, the old man was calm and patient with the child.

"I'm good. It feels nice to stand." Hank's words pleased the old man. He found worth in men that could stay positive. Wars, in his opinion, were won or lost as much by morale as by weapons and tactics.

"I had my eyes closed the whole time. I could hear the fight though. The sizzle of flesh. The cracking of bones. The screaming. I was afraid he was killing you."

"I'm better at killing than dying. Not sure if that's lucky or not, but it seems to be the way of things."

The old man watched Hank's gaze shift to the burning body of his father's killer sticking out from the stove. He snapped his fingers, hoping to call the boy's attention back to him.

"No need to be looking at that. You've had enough unpleasantness."

"Ain't unpleasant. It's right. Like that witch in Hansel and Gretel getting stuffed in the oven."

They both paused for a moment, the only sound being the popping and sizzling of the cannibal's searing flesh.

"It's kind of beautiful, actually."

The old man frowned.

CHAPTER TEN

Two weeks had passed since Emmett crushed the trachea of his part-time employer, Harvey Mackum. Roughly three weeks had gone by since his hateful, dying grandfather had directed him to the *Cavern of The First Breath*. Even for a sixteen-year-old boy, this was no great amount of time. In that short window amazing things had happened, however. Magical things, one might say. Emmett, for one, had no doubt that magic was the right word. It could be nothing else, after all.

"Be a dear Emmett, and pass me another plantain," his mother asked in a pleasant and musical voice that seemed almost strong. The sickness had robbed her voice of its natural, strong, and beautiful tone, and Emmett had believed he'd never hear that voice again. But here it was, taking back its rightful place and exorcising the tired, breathless croak that had come to be associated with his mother in recent months.

The sickness had taken a toll on her. Far more gray was visible in her hair, and her face had aged. But the disease, whatever it had been, was gone now. The healthy, olive color of her skin had returned, washing away the ashen complexion she had worn while death was knocking. She was putting on weight, shrugging off the emaciated, mummified appearance that had marked her in recent weeks.

It was in her eyes that Emmett saw the biggest change. Just a week ago she was ready to die. It had been clear in those brown pools where her soul danced. She had given up. Now there was hope in her eyes. Something else too—desire. Desire to live and breathe. Desire to taste, and touch, and feel, and smell. Desire to love and dance and sing. *And is desire not the secret elixir of life?* Emmett mused.

Emmett watched his mother shovel down fried plantains, and could not help but smile at his work. It was he who had saved her, trading life for life. He was proud of this. He was proud of the fact that he had sought out his grandfather and the secrets that the old man held. He was proud of himself for descending into the dark, cold wetness that was the *Cavern of the First Breath*. Despite not remembering how he had done so, Emmett was even proud of making it back home. Most of all, he was proud of squeezing the very life force out of Harvey Mackum and trading that life force with the lady of the pit, like a pile of ethereal greenbacks.

Emmett stabbed a piece of plantain, and looked deep into his mother's hopeful eyes. He, too, felt hope. Death had been staved off. If that could be done, everything else would surely go back to normal soon. The war would end, and his father would come home. People would buy guns, beautiful one-of-a-kind guns like only his pa could build, and there would never again be a question about where dinner was coming from.

"Now that my appetite's coming back, I'm afraid I'll eat us out of house and home," Emmett's mother said with a laugh. Though she had not meant anything by it, other than to point out how healthy her appetite was becoming, it made Emmett think of one single fact. His father wasn't home yet, and even if the war ended tomorrow morning, he wouldn't be home for some time. This meant that no one would be shelling out a hundred bucks for a fancy new revolver just yet. This, in turn, meant that what little money Emmett had was about to dry up. With Mackum dead and buried in his own orange grove, the fair wages that the bastard had paid were now gone as well.

For the first time it occurred to Emmett that he had not only bitten the hand that fed, but had torn it off. A fear welled up in the pit of his stomach, as heavy and as hot as molten lead. It was a fear that he'd not be able to feed him and his mother, and a fear that such knowledge might send her back over the edge and into the sickness. She was just starting to get better and he was not about to let stress undo the magic he had weaved with Mackum's blood.

"Don't you worry, Ma," Emmett said with a faux smile. "I've been working hard and saving hard."

This was a lie. Emmett had used almost all of the money he'd earned from picking oranges to pay back Mary for watching his ma while he had been off chasing magic. He hadn't dared to steal from Mackum. Somehow he knew that would weaken the power of the sacrifice.

Magic. Maybe that was the answer. The spells that had been burned into his mind by the hides in the cavern were powered by desire and sacrifice. To save his mother's life, the young man had channeled his heart and soul through Mackum's death, striking a deal with death herself. But there were other beings in that icy hell. Dwarfish beings, clad in riches, who no doubt could be bargained with more easily than the hell queen. And if Emmett could wield the power to stave off the disease that had ravaged his mother, could he not call upon magic that would bring him wealth? Surely summoning cash must be simpler than sidestepping oblivion, or so Emmett thought.

With this idea in his mind, Emmett found that the burning fear in his stomach, that molten lead, had seemed to melt away. His mother was alive and well, and now he had the answer to his financial problems—if he could find a suitable trade.

***

Elvis was something of a wanderer. He'd enjoyed playing harmonica, seeing new sights, and the warm feeling brought on by a stiff drink, but not much else. He was dirty and unkempt and cared little what folk thought of him. He had little interest in women and no desire to start a family. His own parents had died when he was but a boy, leaving him without any roots. This left him to follow the good weather, drink beneath the stars, find work where he could, and enjoy the freedom of an unfettered life. If he had lived a few more years, he might have pioneered the railway hobo way of life. This was not to be Elvis's lot. Instead he would die in Affirmation, California, on a night when the stars were right, years before the Central and Union railways would meet and truly unify the continent.

Elvis was not privy to the knowledge of his impending death this night. All he knew was that some easy money had been offered to him. Enough money to keep him in whiskey for the next two months. All he had to do was help some kid rip off his old man's shop. Normally he wouldn't be up for anything risky, but this sounded too easy to pass up. The kid's dad was off fighting in the war between the States, and the kid was left to take care of the gun shop. Evidently the little bastard (well not really little, a moose of a kid, truth be told), couldn't smith a decent piece if his life depended on it. There was some sort of big insurance policy on the equipment there though. The big moosey kid figured that his dad's gun making gear was worth more to him stolen than it was intact.

So the job was like this: Elvis got to move the stolen goods— machinery, guns, ammo—and keep the profit. In return, the kid got his insurance payoff. It was an *everybody wins* kind of job, and a well-paying one at that. Elvis liked it when everybody won. Things always went smoother when everybody stood to make a profit.

It was well past midnight in Affirmation, and no folks were walking the streets, despite the unusually bright starlight. The shine of the stars made Elvis nervous that he'd be seen by some old biddy who was looking out the window because she couldn't sleep. He was right to be nervous of the stars, even if his reasoning was off.

Elvis walked around the gun shop on Palomar Street, trying to be as nonchalant as he could. Stopping in the back of the building, Elvis opened the back door, which was already jimmied ajar as part of the narrative that he and the boy had constructed. Having the kid break it earlier in the night saved Elvis from making noise and attracting unwanted attention.

Elvis stepped through the door. Inside was blackness. The brightness of the night sky threw only slivers of silver light here and there. Elvis stepped inside and stopped, afraid he might trip over something unseen. Instead of stepping further in, Elvis shuffled forward, hoping to bump into any unforeseen obstacles and not tumble over them.

Once he was inside and the door was closed behind him, Elvis fished through his pockets for a box of matches. The kid was supposed to have put all the good stuff, anything worth a damn and easy to sell, into a sack in the middle of the room. All Elvis would have to do was grab it and leave without catching anyone's attention. One match would give him the light he needed to find the sack, and hopefully the brief flicker of light wouldn't be seen by anyone outside.

Elvis pulled out a match and placed the head against the box. Just before he struck the match, less than a second before flame erupted with a tiny pop, Elvis heard a not so tiny click. His mind told him what it was before the light of the match confirmed it, illuminating the gun pointed at his face.

***

Flame popped into existence, almost like an answer to the click of Emmett's revolver. The orange light of the tiny match flame danced eerily across the vagrant's face. Emmett felt this made it harder to see his quarry. The fire had crippled his night vision, replacing it with shaky inconsistent illumination. Even as such, Emmett doubted there would be any problem.

The poor, filthy bastard looked more confused than frightened, like he couldn't quite figure out why there was a change in plans.

No change in plans, partner, Emmett thought, *It's simply time for full disclosure.*

This was wrong, though. The simple sight of the revolver was not full disclosure. There was more to this story than the vagrant would ever know. Symbols, ancient and forgotten runes, older than the memory of any god, were drawn upon the ground with metal shavings. The stars above were aligned in such a way that any other night this year, his eminent death would have been moot.

Emmett pulled the trigger of his revolver, a custom-made piece, modeled after the Dragoon pistol. The bark of lightning filled the night air, and a lead slug cut through the vagrant's neck. He fell to the ground gurgling and choking as blood pooled in his throat. The match fell with him and extinguished. All was darkness now, save for the strands of starlight that could sneak in through the windows and cracks.

While Emmett would need to make a sacrifice tonight, it would not be the vagrant's meager and insignificant life. What use would the denizens of the icy pit have for such a shabby soul? No, the vagrant was not the sacrifice. He had been the key.

The gods of Hell could only be reached by opening the gate between the land of the living and the realm of the dead. Such a gate could be opened solely through death, as a soul travelled from this world to the next. As consciousness drained from the vagrant's mind and lifeblood drained from his throat, the veil between worlds crumbled within the circle of metal shavings. The unimaginable cold of death's realm—that place outside of man's world—blew up from the rough wooden planks that made up the floor of the gun shop (although Emmett was not convinced that the floor of his father's workshop was even there any longer). The hot California air crashed against the cold winds of Hell, creating a white mist that swirled like some tornado of fog.

Emmett felt as if he were floating in the darkness. He could not see his hands, nor the gun in them, nor any part of himself. The dead man in front of him was lost in the shadows as well. For all Emmett knew, his corpse had fallen into the source of the frigid current emanating beneath them. Such a turn of events would prove fortuitous. He would have no body to dispose of and no narrative to spin for the sheriff.

The blood had been spilled and the key turned. Now Emmett needed to speak the words and call upon the being he wished to barter with. Its name had been whispered in his blood. It was a secret knowledge that he thought was passed on surely through the blood of his mother's people.

"Nibelung," Emmett invoked the name in a whisper that held more power than the loudest war cry.

The slivers of starlight that had managed to force their way into the building now began to change direction. Several different beams met within the center of Emmett's circle. At the point where each beam of light departed its natural course, they had transformed into tight rays of brilliant shifting colors. Tiny, terrifying rainbows in the darkness, they illuminated the icy void beneath the circle and drew out the thing that Emmett had summoned.

And so Nibelung rose from the circle, pulled up by prismatic bonds. Its body was humanoid, enormous but stout. Its ten-foot height was matched by the width of its shoulders. The creature's nightmare features and frostbitten skin were only partially illuminated by the shifting axis of light. Still Emmett knew it was the creature from his dream—the dwarf who had beckoned him greedily while he thrashed in the river of slush. The light reflected off of the riches worked into the dwarf's beard and the gaudy rings that bit into its meaty, calloused fingers.

Curtis M. Lawson

Incomprehensible words, the sounds of breaking ice and something being dragged through gravel, erupted from the lips of the thing that Emmett knew as Nibelung. Sane words—words in Emmett's own tongue of Americanized English—echoed through the circle, following the dwarf's guttural barks like some sort of audial Rosetta Stone.

"He who summons Nibelung the betrayer best do so with good reason." The speech had a metallic quality to it, as if the metal shavings that made up the circle had affected the tone.

More barking leapt from the dwarf's mouth—cracking ice and breaking glass and gravel crunching under foot. The alien words were followed immediately by the metallic voice of the circle.

"It was I who first betrayed this world for the lords of Utgard. For that treachery I have eternity at my fingertips and riches more vast than all of the gold created from every star that has ever died."

The barking paused first, then the echoed speech.

After the space of ten seconds the dwarf croaked his inarticulate voice once more, and the surrounding voice followed suit.

"What could one such as you possibly offer one such as me?"

Emmett closed his eyes and inhaled deeply, trying to banish the fear that was clawing its way up his belly. The sterile smell of eternal cold—the smell of *fimblewinter*—flooded his nostrils and made him feel even more panicked.

"I offer this," Emmett spoke in a shaky voice. With a trembling hand he extended the pistol toward Nibelung, with the business end pointed down so as not to threaten or offend the dwarf. The maddening rainbow light bounced off of the gun's chrome barrel and tumblers. The silver inlay of the walnut grip sparkled in the darkness, shifting tone along with the shifting illumination. In the strange light, the acid etched name on the barrel, *Blitzen*, seemed to float above the actual weapon, lending it a phantasmal quality.

"The most finely crafted weapon on this continent," Emmett gulped, noting the thing's head tilt to the side. He prayed that the minimal light would not reveal Nibelung's grotesque face in greater detail. If he were forced to look upon the dwarf in its terrible wholeness he would surely lose his nerve. If that were to happen, Emmett was quite sure he would be joining the vagrant and the dwarf for all time in that arctic nightmare world just beneath his feet.

The shifting light was kind. Nibelung's features, most of them at least, remained veiled in darkness.

"Nothing quite like it in the world," Emmett continued, albeit a bit shakily. "No cocking the hammer. Just pull the trigger and the bullets fly as fast as you can squeeze. Makes the Winston repeater look like a musket."

Nibelung clenched its fist. Sparks lit up the darkness as its ten rings ground against one another. Its barking voice began once more, this time seeming angrier.

The circle translated Nibelung's words in its metallic voice.

"What use have I with such a crude trinket?"

"This pistol is not crude, great Nibelung. Nor is it a trinket."

Emmett placed the gun across his open palms, grimacing at the heat that was still retained in the barrel after shooting the vagrant.

"This is a tool of death, capable of taking six lives in less than that many seconds. It is crafted from the finest steel, finished with a walnut grip, and inlaid with the purest silver. Its name is *Blitzen*, for all great weapons deserve a name, and it was crafted by my father's hands."

Nibelung leaned forward, the cracks in its necrotized face shining with frozen ooze. Its coal black eyes jumped back and forth between the pistol and Emmett's own eyes. Emmett held the creature's gaze, even as he felt the madness in its mind transferring to his own.

"It's the greatest treasure I have to give. A one-of-a-kind gift from my pa. The most advanced pistol on earth, so far as I know."

Nibelung reached out its massive hand and took the pistol from Emmett's outstretched palms. *Blitzen* disappeared into the dwarf's grip.

With its other hand, the creature called Nibelung, amongst other names, ran four thick fingers through its course beard. Coins and rings of gold rained from the dwarf's face and clattered upon the floor that seemed not to be there.

The creature croaked one final word in that terrible voice. This time the circle did not translate. Emmett was sure that this alien word meant their business was concluded.

Confirming Emmett's thoughts, the beams of prismatic light exploded into a brilliant flash. He was left momentarily blind from the intensity of the light. When the world began to reform before his eyes, it had lost the eldritch elements that had dominated it only moments ago. The arctic chill was gone, along with the yawning hell-mouth from which it had erupted. The terrible rainbow lights had vanished, or perhaps simply reverted into the slivers of silver moonlight. Through one sliver of moonlight, Emmett could see that seals that marked his circle were now scorched, but intact. All else was darkness.

"The circle is opened," Emmett muttered, "but never broken."

He stumbled through the darkness and beyond the diameter of his place of summoning. He blindly searched for the oil lamp that he had earlier placed on the shop's counter. Finally finding it, Emmett struck a match and set flame to the oil-soaked wick. It caught fire and filled the room with a soft yellow radiance.

In the lamplight Emmett now saw that the vagrant's body was indeed gone, presumably fallen into the gate that had been opened, or perhaps burned away into nothingness after he served as the key. Whatever the case, Emmett was glad to see the body gone. One less thing he would have to clean up or explain away. One less terrible image to haunt his dreams.

The magic circle was outlined with black, green, and umber shavings of steel and copper that had burned and oxidized during the ceremony. In the center of the circle was a pile of gold—coins the size of Spanish doubloons. The coins were mixed among gold and silver rings with mysterious characters inscribed upon them. Emmett tried to estimate the worth of what he was seeing, finally settling upon the simple answer. He had just become very, very wealthy.

He wasted no time getting to work cleaning up the metal shavings, effectively dismantling his summoning circle, and weighing his newfound riches on the scale that his father used for rationing out black powder. He worked in dim light, hoping not to draw any undue attention. The gunshot that had ended a life and opened the gate to Hell had not been quiet though. It had awoken several neighbors. The one who had thought enough of it and cared enough to check up on it was, as luck would have it, the man whom Emmett wanted to see the least under current circumstances.

A knock came from the front door, causing Emmett to jump and spill a gold coin to the floor. To his relief the soft metal produced only a dull thud upon impact with the wooden floor. He had been expecting some loud clang, as if the gold were cursed and bent on securing him into hands of the law.

"We're closed," Emmett shouted as he shuffled the dwarven riches underneath the counter.

"Emmett, it's Sheriff Silver. Can I come in?"

"Oh. Uhmm, yeah, of course." Emmett tried to keep a calmness to his voice. He was sure he was failing in that regard.

"Just gimme a second to unlock the door."

A quick glance around revealed nothing that might implicate him in the crimes that he had just committed. No body on the floor, nor pools of blood. No arcane symbols to make anyone think of witchcraft. No stray gold to raise suspicions.

Emmett unlocked and opened the front door to the shop. He met Sheriff Silver, who was perhaps a full foot shorter than Emmett, with a curious glance.

"Evening, Sheriff," Emmett said, more as a question than a statement.

"Everything all right, Emmett?"

Emmett swallowed hard before replying. "Yeah. Absolutely, sir."

Silver eyed the young man suspiciously and spoke "Heard the crack of gunfire. Woke my ass outta dead sleep. Sounded like it came from here."

Fear overcame Emmett, deeper than the terror evoked by Nibelung's ghastly visage. It was that childish fear of getting in trouble. Somehow this mortal man, whom Emmett outweighed and outmuscled, was putting a mighty fear into him more intense than a literal monster had done moments before. In many ways Emmett was immature for his age which served to his advantage when mentally processing the inhuman powers that he now courted. This immaturity lent a stronger belief in the perceived authority of adults though, particularly adults with badges. A man like Silver could still hold a strong sway over him.

"I'm mighty sorry about the noise. Was making some cartridge rounds and must have put too much powder in one."

Emmett watched Silver's face, trying to read whether he was buying it. If the man knew the first thing about making ammunition then his story was blown. Silver seemed blank and expressionless. Emmett couldn't read him worth a damn.

"Lucky I didn't lose a hand," Emmett followed up after an uncomfortable moment of silence.

"Strange hours to be making ammo."

"Yeah," Emmett replied. "Couldn't sleep though, and figured it'd be smart to build some surplus. Been selling more bullets since they found Mackum's body."

Emmett immediately cursed himself for bringing up the dead farmer. Silver was going to figure it all out, just like some hotshot penny dreadful detective.

"Folks are nervous. Guns and ammo are a good medicine for nervousness," Emmett said, following up his last thought.

"Hmmm," Silver replied as he slipped into the shop, right past Emmett's massive form. The lawman was scanning the area, his eyes running across the counter, the display cases, the walls, and floors. Emmett hoped that if he'd missed some tiny bit of evidence that it would stay hidden by the shifting shadows produced by the oil lamp's unsteady flame.

The sheriff stopped, right in the middle of where the circle had been, and reached a hand into his shirt pocket. Emmett's heart raced a thousand beats per minute. He knew Silver was a Jew, and according to some folks, the sons of Israel had magic of their own, just as dark as Emmett's. What if Silver could sense the residual energy of Nibelung's summoning? What if God, being an admittedly envious lord, had keyed Silver in about Emmett's dealings with the gods of the pit?

All that Silver produced from his pocket was a cigarette case. He pulled out a smoke and placed the tin case back into his shirt pocket.

Emmett's fear eased a bit.

"Well you be careful, and let's save any potentially explosive work for the morning. You hear?"

Emmett nodded, dry-mouthed.

The lawman pointed his unlit cigarette in the massive teenager's direction and smiled.

"I don't want you waking me up again," Silver's tone was friendly enough, but Emmett felt that the friendliness was insincere.

The sheriff pulled his hand back toward his mouth and fumbled his cigarette. The paper-wrapped tobacco tumbled end over end, landing on the wood floor that had been displaced by the cold winds of Hell not long ago.

"See that, boy? You got me so tired I can't even keep a grip on my tobacco." Silver's tone was friendly once again abut insincerity still crept out from beneath that gregarious tone.

Bending at the knees, his eyes staying on Emmett the whole time, Silver reached down and grabbed his cigarette, this time holding it between his thumb and forefinger, so that it faced into his palm.

"You get some sleep, kid," Silver said, extending his hand out in Emmett's direction.

Emmett took the lawman's delicate hand, a shootist's hand, in his own massive bear paw. They shook and Emmett let the sheriff out through the front door. Once Silver was gone Emmett threw the lock and fell on his ass against the door.

His heartbeat slowed and he took in deep breaths. Silver was gone and he was none the wiser. Emmett had gotten away with murder for the second time and now he had everything he needed. His mother was healthy and he was wealthy. A wide smile crossed Emmett's face and he began to laugh in relief.

There were things of course that Emmett didn't know—things that would have crushed that sense of relief. He didn't realize that Silver, being a perceptive bastard, had spied the dark red gunk between the shop's floorboards, something Emmett himself had missed in the dim light of the oil lamp. Nor was the young man aware that the Sheriff had dropped his cigarette on purpose, in order to soak a sample of that same red gunk into the paper. He certainly had no idea that Silver already suspected him in Mackum's death and had a gut suspicion that the crimson between the boards was gore.

CHAPTER ELEVEN

Many a story and poem evoke the beauty of the western sky
at night. The old man had grown to distrust the stars though. Where
others saw beacons in a sea of darkness, he gleaned the fires of an
advancing army. What men of faith called the heavens, the old man
called Utgard—that which lies outside.

The earthly place in that he and Hank now walked through
mirrored the sky in some ways. Like the malevolent stars above, it
was a living and wicked thing, defying the wasteland that
surrounded it. Tanner's grove, so named for the single tree jutting
forth out of the cracked clay, was an "end-of-track town." Dozens
like it had popped up and vanished just as fast, following the
procession of Union Rail workers. Each in its turn sat at the edge of
the world, until the world grew a bit larger.

Today, the edge of the world was three hundred miles west of
Omaha.

Three hours had passed since the day had started anew, but
Tanner's Grove was wide awake. Tents and shanties of every
conceivable purpose littered the wasteland around the rails. An all-
in-one house of vice—booze, opium, gambling, whores—occupied a
massive and elaborate tent next to a doctor who specialized in
venereal diseases.

Another large tent lay farther from the tracks with a massive cross posted outside of it as a beacon to repentant sinners. Men of more mundane occupations—blacksmiths, carpenters, bakers—had set up shop as well. All were eager to cash in on the railroad.

The old man wondered how the workers managed to burn the candle at both ends the way that they did. Rail work was hard and dangerous, not the kind of thing to undertake with last night's whiskey still on your breath.

The old man's eyes darted between the house of sin and the house of God. Both were places of passion and power. Both could sway the hearts of men. If the thing called Thurs had set up shop in Tanner's Grove, it would be as a master of either spirit or flesh.

The old man decided to try the makeshift church, only because he'd rather face the beast there. It was clear that less folks were interested in praying than boozing. The old man was holding out hope that if iron had to be drawn, then collateral damage could be limited.

The drunks and whores in the street paid little attention to him, despite his unusual size. One particularly observant rail worker repeatedly shifted his eyes between the old man's Confederate jacket and the dark-skinned boy who travelled with him.

"Stay close," he muttered to Hank, not expecting the Negro orphan to fare well on his own around this rough element. The two had traveled together for months after the incident in the mountains. They'd made it through the Sierra Nevada, crossed the Utah desert, and skirted the Rockies up into Wyoming before meeting up with the railroad in Nebraska. The old man, despite having made a few half-hearted attempts to leave Hank with more respectable folk, had grown quite fond of the boy.

Across the tracks from where they stood the church's giant wooden cross loomed like a symbol of Roman terror, rather than an icon of human hope. Even in the dark, the instrument of Christ's end cast a shadow. The old man had no fear of stepping through the shadow of death, nor of god. Gods were titanic things after all, and one could only slay them from within their eclipse.

Hank, on the other hand, shivered at the image of the cross, recalling the writhing wooden effigy that had served as council to his father's killer. Walking in its shadow, the boy's blood chilled within his veins.

The old man ducked down a bit as he entered the canvas church, then held the flap open for Hank. Inside, it was completely black. No moon, nor hateful stars, nor burning lantern dared penetrate this nomadic holy of holies.

The old man struck a match. Sulfur and fire erupted with a puff of white smoke, forcing back just enough darkness to see a few inches ahead. An educated guess and some feeling around brought the old man to an oil lantern that sat near the entrance of the tent. The flame had nearly consumed his match and was threatening his flesh as he ignited the wick on the lantern.

Now a larger globe of light surrounded the old man and his companion. He picked up the lantern and turned, hearing a rustle of cloth behind them.

"Hello?" The voice sounded hoarse and there was a tiredness to it. Not the kind of tired that comes from an honest day's work, but an exhaustion of the mind. The old man understood this kind of tired. He'd felt that way since the final days of the war, and it had only gotten worse upon returning home.

A middle-aged priest shifted to a sitting position in his cot, which was propped up in front of the altar. He cast a nervous look toward the stranger in his tent.

"Sorry, my son," the priest said with an inkling of fear in his voice. "While sin never sleeps in Tanner's Grove, the servants of the Lord still must."

"I'm looking for something," the old man said in a dry and quiet drawl as he turned to face the priest. "Reckoned it might be in here."

The priest had misunderstood his meaning. He now mistook the old man for a lost lamb, and his initial fear vanished. A practiced expression of welcoming and pity emerged on the priest's face. It was amazing to the old man how quickly and seamlessly this steward of the cross could shift from nervous rabbit to snake oil salesman.

"I reckon you're right. Sit, my son," the priest motioned toward a row of nearby chairs.

Lantern in hand, the old man walked toward the priest. The shifting lantern light caused shadows to dance across his form and left the old man with a wraithlike countenance. Hank followed like the shadow of a ghost.

The old man stayed quiet for a moment. He eyed the priest, spiritually sizing him up. After an awkwardly long silence, the priest cleared his throat and spoke.

"Hope you don't mind me saying, but my, you are a big one. Gotta be tall as Lincoln and twice as wide."

"Suppose that's accurate," the old man said as he sat down.

"I see you fought for Davis," The priest said, gesturing to the old man's jacket. "I can see the hardness of war ingrained in your face. The horror of battle and the sorrow of defeat weigh heavy on your soul. They've aged you beyond your years"

The old man said nothing. He simply watched the holy man's eyes for the flicker of madness that marked union with those beyond.

"That anger and pain, it can come to feel like home. When you think you have nothing left, it's there for you. But that black comfort is the devil's hand, and it will kill you, my son."

The old man kept silent and stared into the priest's eyes for another moment. The man may have prayed to them through the proxy of the cross, but the Devourers had not touched his mind. At least not directly. The old man was satisfied that the priest was no witch.

"The war was…unkind to me. No doubt about that. I watched a lot of good men die. I'm sure I killed quite a few good men myself."

The old man cracked his neck and resumed speaking. "That's all blood under the bridge though. Nowadays I'm just trying to get home. Figuratively, that is."

Thoughts of another time, a better time, left a faraway look in the old man's eyes.

"And your companion?" The priest gestured toward Hank, who was clinging nervously to the old man's coat.

"Boy's an orphan. Just getting him to a safe place."

"The Lord can ease that pain and guide you home, if you let him. That goes for both of you."

"More like if I make him," the old man thought aloud, still daydreaming of days before presidents, armies, witches, and gods had torn his life to shreds.

"Excuse me?" the priest replied, doing little to hide his outrage. "One does not force the Lord to do anything, my son."

The old man snapped out of his reverie, but refused to acknowledge the priest's indignation.

"Don't wanna waste no more of your time, Padre. Looks like you ain't selling what I'm looking for."

The priest frowned.

"Trust me, that ain't a bad thing," the old man replied to the priest's unspoken disappointment.

The old man tipped his hat, turned, and walked toward the tent's egress with Hank in tow. As his hand pulled back the flap that led to the outside world, the old man stopped for a minute. He turned his head and spoke a question to his host.

"Guessing you been following the hell on wheels for a stretch. Ain't never heard of a thing what calls itself Thurs, have you, Padre? A nightmare parading itself as a man? Big as a mustang with skin like cracked Nevada clay?"

The priest stared at the old man with an expression that merged fear, pity, and surprise. Either the priest thought the old man mad, or he had crossed paths with the creature at one time. The old man took the priest's silent expression as a yes.

"That thing here now?"

The priest opened his mouth to form an answer. Before any sound could escape, the deafening thunder of rifle fire erupted outside. The gun shots were followed by the distinctive war cries of Cheyenne raiders.

The old man closed the distance between himself and the priest. He pulled his host low to the ground to avoid gun fire.

"Father, is Thurs in Tanner's grove?"

The priest made the sign of the cross and closed his eyes in fear.

"This is because you mentioned him! Speak of the devil and he shall appear!"

"Those ain't devils, Padre. Just a bunch of pissed off, scared kids. One ain't got nothing to do with the other."

The old man's terse impatience did nothing to calm the quaking priest. "Now tell me, where the hell is Thurs?"

Tears began to stream down the priest's face and a look of madness encroached in his eyes. The old man doubted that speaking the name of his enemy had summoned the Indian raiders. The mention of the dark titan set against the disquieting Cheyenne howls had certainly invoked a fearful lunacy in the priest, however.

With strong arms and short patience, he tried to shake the priest free of terror. The grip of fear held strong against the old man's prodding. It was clear that the priest would be of no further use, at least not until things had calmed down outside.

He could have waited out the raid inside the tent and simply protected the priest. He could have escaped, dragging the man of god with him to safety. Those options would have taken more time though, and the old man had something of a temporal deficit. Though it had been nearly half a year since Thurs had taken his boy, he still saw each second as precious. Every tick of the clock lessened the chances of him saving his son.

Leaving the priest to shake and piss, the old man drew iron and exited the tent. The primitive song of war cries and gunfire had increased in tempo. Screams of fear and howls of pain joined the cacophonous symphony. The old man readied his instrument, the revolver he had smithed himself, and joined the chorus.

The old man was at home amongst the sounds of war. Chaos could instill a shakiness in some men, but the old man's nerves were steady. He rested his sights on the charging horse beneath the closest brave. The first of six rounds exploded from his gun's muzzle, finding its mark in equine flesh. The native's steed tumbled to the ground, crushing his rider's leg beneath it.

Another nearby raider was too slow to pull his horse to a stop. The animal's legs caught against the fallen horse in front of it, causing another brave and steed to crash into the sun-baked earth. Eighteen Indians remained.

Few of the braves had noticed the old man yet. Their sights were locked on easier prey. Bullets ripped through the flesh of stumbling drunks. Flint arrowheads tied to flaming shafts set tents aflame. Tomahawks powered by muscles like steel cable cleaved into skulls.

There was one Indian amongst the war party who showed a marked disinterest in the wholesale slaughter around him. His dress placed him apart from the rest of the war party. The braves were stripped down for combat—loin cloths, war paint, and weapons. This man, in contrast, was burdened with numerous talismans and pouches. While the Cheyenne warriors howled with hatred and lust for blood, his face was calm and uninterested in the carnage about him. His dark eyes scanned the chaos, in search of something or someone specific.

The old man locked eyes with the shaman and each recognized the true nature of the other. It was a cruel epiphany for the old man, realizing the priest had been right. The devil's name had been spoken, and here the devil rode toward him, albeit in proxy.

A cruel smirk crossed the face of the medicine man and he charged his horse toward the old man. While in mid-charge he plucked a dark feather from his own hair. At the same time, the old man inhaled and rested his aim on the Indian's center mass.

Both held their breath as they let their missiles take flight. Before the shaman's feather-dart had made it a foot from his hand, the lead slug had already torn through his lungs and lodged into a rib. The Indian was dead before his own weapon could find its mark, but find its mark it would.

The shaft of the feather lodged itself into the old man's left shoulder. The pain was incredible. It burned beneath his flesh, as if the feather were pumping brimstone straight into his muscle and marrow. It didn't much matter to him if it was sorcery or poison—he couldn't die just yet.

With a swift motion, he plucked the feather from his shoulder, hoping to cut off the flow of agony that was filling him. He flung it to the ground and stumbled backward. Raising his gun, which seemed to have grown a bit heavier, the old man found his sight too blurred to aim. The world flipped on its side and the old man was suddenly hit by the earth itself.

Darkness crept into his blurred field of vision, starting at the center of his view and spreading out like ink in water. The sounds of the world—screams, gunshots, and pounding hooves—faded shortly after his sight of it.

CHAPTER TWELVE

Life was good. Emmett's ma was healthy as a lark and had been for months. The savory aroma of her cooking was now ever-present. Money had ceased to be a concern. The house was full of laughter and light.

And, perhaps best of all, folks were saying the war would be over soon. It wasn't looking good for the Confederacy, but what did it matter which side won, so long as his pa made it home? Only months before, Emmett had understood and supported his father's decision to don the gray war garb of the southern states. Now the whole conflict seemed petty and childish to him. Was there really a difference between North and South? They had both stolen this country from its true people.

Yes, life was good. Something gnawed at Emmett's mind and soul however, keeping him awake at night. It wasn't guilt, as one might expect from a young man who'd twice murdered. Nor was it the patches of dry skin or the nightmares he suffered. What kept Emmett awake at night and what haunted him during the day was the sense that he had stumbled upon the threshold of the infinite. He had glimpsed the divine, yet was still bound by gravity, mortality, and legality. He had walked the lands of the dead and saw that there was something beyond even those icy plains. He wanted more than a glimpse.

The knowledge from the skins held within the *Cavern of the First Breath,* the formulae and ancient secrets that had been burned into his mind, and the magic that had made a rich man of him and saved his mother's life seemed somehow weak and elementary now. Yes, the power he had attained and the wicked might he wielded dwarfed the greatest accomplishments of science, but Emmett's field of vision had expanded. He knew that greater power and infinite wisdom could be gleaned if he could just tap into the deeper vistas of reality—into the worlds that lay outside.

The problem that Emmett now faced was that he had become a student with no master. What strides he had made in the dark arts were the result of exposure to a single set of documents and an innate intuition. While he had an awareness that other worlds existed, he knew not how to reach any beyond the realm of death.

It was with this dilemma in mind that Emmett had returned to the Paiute reservation two weeks prior. His grandfather, the dying old medicine man, would share his secrets with Emmett. Of course he might refuse at first, but Emmett would convince him. He would reason first. If reason failed he would beg. If begging proved fruitless he would resort to more aggressive forms of persuasion. Of course, the other natives might come to his grandfather's aid if things got violent, but Emmett felt that the potential gain was worth the risk.

On arriving at the reservation, Emmett found that all his plans had been dashed. Hateful old Poohwi had died in his sleep two nights prior, under the dark sky of a new moon. Perhaps it was unreasonable, but Emmett felt as if the old bastard had died on purpose, leaving his hated half-breed grandson to suffer with knowledge of power he could never grasp.

There was another shaman in the camp. He was younger and had a kindness in his eyes that Emmett found to be a rarity in this world. Desperate for any knowledge that might take him up the next rung on the ladder of eternity, Emmett had tried to pry any information he could from the young shaman. There was a sternness in the native equal to his kindness, and he refused to give Emmett that which he sought. Something told Emmett that the young man would not be bullied and that a confrontation would lead to less than desirable results.

Instead, the young shaman, apprentice to hateful Poohwi, left Emmett with an unwelcome insight.

"Poohwi was mad in his old age, made wicked by his anger," he explained. "He did an awful thing to you, sending you that forsaken pit and damning you with that dark wisdom. Worse still, he was trying to do an awful thing to the whole world."

The shaman stopped speaking and locked eyes with Emmett, waiting to see if he yet understood. After several seconds he realized that Emmett had not.

"He burdened you with those dark secrets so that you might open the pathway."

"What pathway?" Emmett asked, feeling confident that he already knew the answer.

"The pathway to the black places between the stars. The path that leads to those that lie outside. Or more accurately, the path that leads them to us."

Emmett's heart raced as the young man spoke of those spheres beyond the world he knew. The dry patches of skin on his body began to itch and burn, as if mention of those secret paths had excited something beneath. His mind reeled in two voices. One voice cried out for the power and thrill offered by some exotic realm outside of this existence. A second voice, one that Emmett could not recognize as his own, bellowed with excitement at the prospect of a road that might lead out from the suffocating oceans of darkness.

The young shaman could read the excitement plainly on Emmett's face. In turn, his own face became a mask of sadness.

"Your grandfather has poisoned you. He has poisoned your mind, body, and soul. He has stricken you with a lust for the gifts of evil spirits. Worse still, he hoped to poison the whole world through you."

Emmett laughed. It was a cynical but sincere laugh. The laugh of a teenager who scoffs when told that his actions can hold the power change the world.

"Poison the whole world, huh? Mighty ambitious. Reckon he must have been going senile though, hinging his hopes on the half-breed son of a gunsmith."

"This is no joke. The magic you toy with, the spirits you invoke—these things could end mankind. The nameless one who breathed the first breath, he is a spirit of ravenous hunger. Poohwi wanted you to release him so that he could devour this world, just as the white man devoured ours."

"So why not release the spirit himself, if that was the case?"

"Because he was afraid, and he was wise in his fear. Even in the closing days of his life, Poohwi chose to die as himself, rather than live as a vessel for that monstrous thing."

And so Emmett had left the Paiute reservation, scoffing at the warnings of the young shaman and cursing the grandfather who had died to spite him. He traveled home low with disappointment, but far from defeated. There were other sources of wisdom in this world— other learned men and women that might lead him to the knowledge he sought.

Now, two weeks after his second pilgrimage to Bishop Colony, Emmett was readying to make his way out on a new pilgrimage to a town called Emerald. Stories had gotten around about a brothel outside of Emerald where one of the whores would read your fortune with an eerie accuracy.

Folks who passed through town would often spend a few hours in Tom Porter's saloon, and many of them vouched for the spot-on nature of the fortunes gleaned by the whore seer. If what these passing drunks claimed was to be trusted, then this witch might just be his huckleberry. Yes, a witch was exactly what he needed.

Before heading southwest to Emerald, he'd have to concoct some lie to tell his ma. That would be simple enough. Emmett hadn't shared with her the fact that they were rich. He had no reasonable way to explain the plentiful amounts of gold and silver that were hidden beneath the floorboards of his bedroom, nor did he want to draw any attention from Sheriff Silver, who had taken a keen interest in him since the night he'd summoned Nibelung. To avoid concern from either party, Emmett had been leaving town for a day or two at a time. He'd claim to have taken on odd jobs at nearby farms, or work as muscle for teamsters that needed a hand loading and unloading carts. As far as Emmett could tell, this narrative seemed to satisfy any concern his mother might have and any suspicion in the mind of the sheriff.

On this particular night, two nights before he would depart and seek out the whore oracle, Emmett enjoyed perhaps the most pleasant night he could remember since his father up and left them for the blood-soaked fields of war. His mother had made a dinner of spiced carrots with roasted potatoes and pheasant. Her beauty and grace shined through her smile. She laughed and joked and told old stories about her and his father. The mundane conversation of his parent's early romance, and comedic stories about himself as a child pushed away the darkness that had recently taken up so much real estate in Emmett's mind. Dreams of re-lived murder faded behind the atavistic power of dinner's aroma. Yearnings for otherworldly power were forgotten in the musical laughter of his mother's voice. The itching of his cracked, dry skin (eczema, the doctor had called it), subsided in their shared hope that his father might return shortly.

Soon the subject turned to Emmett himself and his own future. His mother was beyond hopeful for him. She saw in his eyes, eyes so much like his father's, tenderness tempered with strength, traits that would do him well in this world. She also saw fear. Once again it was the same fear that his father was burdened with. She told him as much on this night.

"You're so strong, Emmett," she said, taking his hand in her own from across the table. "So much like your pa."

This statement invoked a mixture of emotions within Emmett, which he was not mature or introspective enough to understand. The insinuation that he was growing into a man like his father triggered currents of doubt and shadows of pride, for his father was the strongest and smartest man he'd ever known. It also churned up a tumult of conceited anger. He wasn't, in truth, like his father at all. He had stayed home and saved his ma from death's cold grip.

Last, this comparison brought to mind what he considered the greatest difference between he and his father. His pa found solace in the empirical world and saw the sharp mind of man as the alpha and omega. He remembered his father once saying that the testimony of humanity's greatness was also its greatest folly—the creation of God. Meanwhile, Emmett now knew from experience that there were things just outside the light that were far greater and more terrible than man. Forgotten powers more deadly than all the artillery in all the world's armies dwelled in spheres of reality far more important than our own.

His father was a self-driven materialist who had found the divine in the touch of a woman and the blast of black powder. Emmett, on the other hand, was a spiritualist who called upon the divine forces of those that lie outside as a tool to manipulate the world.

Emmett's thoughts were not this well formulated however, nor was he even aware that he was thinking them. His conscious mind only knew that he felt angry, proud, and afraid all at once, and it was not trained to look for deeper reasons, so it didn't.

"You're strong, modest, and hard working. There's a barrel load of anger in you though, Emmett. No surprise, given your pa running off to war and me being a burden on you."

"You were never a burden, Ma," Emmett replied, a bit louder than he had intended to.

"Shush. We both know that ain't true," she said, shaking her head. "Anger can be a killer. Your pa is overwhelmed with it, and that's half the reason he's off killing Yankees instead of eating dinner with us. My own father was absolutely sick with it."

Emmett nodded, fully aware that his grandfather had been an angry, evil bastard. His expression, he thought, might have given something away. For a moment he thought his mother might have gleaned some insight, as though his nod had expressed too much firsthand knowledge. Then she continued, and Emmett figured it was just his imagination.

"Like your pa and your granddaddy, you have a bit of fear in you, too." She said this while raising her hands up in an apologetic gesture. "Now there ain't no shame in that. Everyone's afraid. If anger was half the reason your pa went off to fight, fear is the other half. What is important is how you deal with that fear. Your pa owns his fear. He bridles it and whips it and uses it like a mustang to drive him through life. My pa, on the other hand, his fear was a wildfire that burned away his soul and any happiness he ever knew."

Emmett only nodded, not knowing quite what to say. His mother went on.

"It's easy to figure out how to use your love and compassion. It's easy to put strength and hard work to use for you. What's hard— what decides the type of man you are—is whether you use that hate and fear or whether it uses you."

CHAPTER THIRTEEN

The world materialized far more slowly than it had vanished. Nightmare visions of battlefields and failure melted into a mental haze, retaining only enough power to distort the old man's perception of the conscious realm. Dying screams and creaking ice echoed in his mind, making the real-life voices of those nearby barely perceptible. Shrapnel, smoke, and blood splatter were fading from his vision, but reality still hid behind the smokescreen of unconsciousness.

"I think he's waking up." The voice was distant, but the excitement behind it was unmistakable. The old man thought the voice sounded vaguely familiar.

Struggling against his uncooperative muscles, the old man tried to shake his head and banish the foggy remnants of his nightmares. Something in the back of his mind was screaming though, warning him that the nightmare was preferable to reality. But there was something to do in the real world. Someone needed him.

"He may be delirious when he comes to," a stranger's voice echoed. It sounded closer than the familiar voice. Much older as well. The first voice must have been a child's. Was it his son?

"Give him some space," the older voice echoed once more. His son, he remembered—his son needed him.

"Just die, for fuck's sake!" dual voices screamed in his mind. One was his own. The other was a guttural growl that could not be mistaken as human.

His muscles gave up their resistance against his brain, and the old man's head shook back and forth. He opened his eyes to reveal a blurry stranger in a brown jacket, set against a sepia backdrop. The smell of grain alcohol and formaldehyde attacked his nostrils, helping to draw him out from the dream world.

"Relax, friend," the stranger's voice spoke again, this time with less reverb. "That Injun poison's gonna leave ya loopy for a while. Even a big guy like you."

Suddenly the old man remembered everything. His search for his boy, the priest who'd seen Thurs, the Cheyenne raid.

His mind, still foggy from the poison, immediately flooded with questions.

How long had he been out?

Where was he now?

What happened to the priest?

Was Hank okay?

A jumble of nonsense escaped the old man's mouth as he tried to speak. His tongue, like his other muscles, was reluctant to do his will.

The stranger replied with a shush. Somewhere outside of his field of vision, the familiar voice, which he now placed as Hank's, asked if he was okay.

With great effort the old man moved his tongue around in his mouth, noting that it was as dry as the ground in Tanner's Grove. He tried to summon some saliva into his mouth, and was met with minimal response. Regardless, he tried speaking again.

"The ... priest?" The words were more of an inquisitive croak than a proper question.

"Afraid he didn't make it. One of the savages went straight for the mission."

The old man had been afraid that this would be the case.

"He a friend of yours?" the stranger, whom the old man was beginning to place as a doctor, asked.

The old man shook his head to communicate a negative, thankful that he needn't answer verbally.

"Well don't worry, you won't be needing a priest just yet, fella. We do need to have a talk when you're more with it though."

It was then that the old man realized he was shirtless, and could not feel his gun belt digging into his lower back.

He forced a painful, dry gulp before looking over toward Hank.

"My guns?" he asked the boy.

"I got you covered," Hank responded, gesturing to a pile of the old man's personal effects on the clay floor of the doctor's tent.

There was a relieved smile on the boy's face. While it felt nice to have someone look at him with affection for the first time in years, the smile also filled him with a guilty sadness. Despite what they'd been through in the mountains, the boy was hitching his cart to the wrong horse. The road he traveled was one of madness and sorrow. No path for a child.

For the next thirty minutes or so, the old man just lay there, waiting for the poison to lose its grip. The doctor had gone about some other work. Hank had moved his chair so that he was sitting right next to the old man, but made no further sound. Outside, the silence of trauma had settled over the town.

Finally, the old man felt in control of his body again, and most of the haze had burned from his mind. Still distrustful of the line of communication between his body and mind, he forced himself into a sitting position. From this position, he surveyed his body for damage.

A bandage was taped over his shoulder where the Cheyenne dart had struck him during the recent battle. To his relief there were no other serious abrasions or broken bones. On the back of his hand, where the burn from the cannibal's stove had left him with a black scar that spider-webbed out in all directions, the old man was shaken to see a leech attached. Instinctively he swung his hand back and forth, trying to fling the creature from his flesh.

"You're gonna want to keep her on a little bit longer," the doctor said, looking over his shoulder as he checked on another victim of the recent firefight.

The doctor finished whatever it was he was doing with his other patient and walked back toward the old man. He wiped blood from his hands with a stained rag, and set his eyes on the leech that suckled at the old man.

"The Injun's poison, while it could have killed you, is mostly outta yer system," he said, pointing toward the blackened scar tissue at that the leech suckled upon. "That right there is yer real problem."

A grim feeling came over the old man as he looked at the black stain on his skin. He had tried to ignore it up until now, chalking the discoloration up to the burn he'd received. The color and the spider-webbing was something he'd seen before, and he didn't want to think about it. It was the same kind of wretched infection that had been eating away at so many of the witches he'd slain. A physical symptom of the dark magic coursing through their bodies.

"I've never seen anything quite like it. Some kind of infection, and signs of blood poisoning. That's bad enough, but the color ..."

The old man only grunted in response. His mind was too busy sizing up his sickness to offer any other words. This infection, *black vein* he called it, was typically slowed by the same dark powers that spawned it. The old man was no witch though, and knew not the secret ways to slow the sickness.

"I'm hoping that leeches will slow the progress, but ..."

"But what?" Hank, who had been so quiet that he'd been almost forgotten, chimed in. Fear and heartbreak were creeping into his voice.

The old man reached over and placed one hand on Hank's knee, trying his best to comfort the boy.

"How long?" the old man asked, working out the math in his mind of how long it might take to track Thurs down along the railroad.

"A few weeks, I reckon. Maybe two months with leeches and prayer each day."

The old man nodded and swung his feet off the cot.

"But there's gotta be something right?" Hank asked with desperation in his voice. "Some medicine or something?"

A solemn expression came across the doctor's face. "My condolences."

"How much for the leeches?" the old man asked as he pushed off of the cot and gathered his gear.

***

Hank followed the old man closely, unsure what to do or say. He supposed that he knew they were temporary companions, but the thought of the reaper coming for the old man so soon after both of his parents had died was too much for him.

His sullenness at word of the old man's impending death was shaken a bit by fear as they once again crossed under the shadow of the cross and into the chapel tent. Even in the light of day, the wooden "t" seemed to be a thing of evil. The priest was dead, murdered by Indians. It seemed wrong, and somehow dangerous, to enter God's house after his servant had been cut down. The old man showed no fear though, so Hank acted as bravely as he could.

Light poured into the tent, both through the flaps and penetrating through the canvas. A large, amorphous stain adorned the earthen floor of the chapel. To his relief, someone had taken the priest's corpse away. Brutal images of some Cheyenne warrior carving up the holy man came into his mind. He imagined the sharpened stone of a tomahawk cutting the scalp away from the man of God. His mind played out a scene of all-out butchery, where the Indian dressed the priest like a deer. The murderer in Hank's mind had the same clinical detachment that the mountain man had shown when butchering his father.

Hank scanned the room, his young imagination creating a narrative around the blood splatter and general disarray. The priest had caught the tomahawk in the gut, judging by the shit mixed in with the blood. The trail of blood, curving back and forth like a drunk snake, showed where the priest had stumbled in a vain attempt to escape. The rusty blob on the clay floor marked the point of failure, where Padre's body called it quits.

Nothing else seemed disturbed though. A foot locker stowed near the cot was locked and undisturbed. The gold and silver candlesticks hadn't been looted. Even a stash of booze that had fallen out from the overturned altar had been left where it had fallen. The lack of opportunism was a sure sign that the Cheyenne raiders had come to Tanner's Grove for the express purpose of silencing the priest.

"What are we doing here?" Hank finally asked after surveying the grim scene for a moment.

"Hunting," the old man responded as he pulled his secondary revolver from his belt.

The old man cocked his gun and aimed it at the lock on the foot locker. Hank covered his ears, wondering if it was such a good idea to be firing a gun in here so shortly after the Cheyenne raid.

An explosion escaped the old man's pistol and the lock shattered. Wasting no time, the old man bent down and opened the foot locker. He began rifling through the priest's personal effects, looking for some tell-tale sign of where he might have crossed paths with Thurs.

Hank watched the entrance of the tent nervously. The gunshot would surely cause someone to come investigate what was going on. The boy could only imagine what it would look like. They'd be hanged as thieves, stealing from the church itself. And what better people could they find for hanging than a Confederate soldier and Negro orphan. Not only were both widely hated, but what a funny story it would make for the lynch mob to tell down the road.

"I shit you not, a god damn nigger-boy, and some Dixie land hold over were thieving together. Quite a funny sight, swinging side by side," That's what they'd say alright.

Before Hank's anxiety could mount any further, the old man shot upright, holding several train tickets and a journal in his hand. In the other hand was a fistful of greenbacks.

"Got what I need," the old man said in his ever-calm tone.

"Taking from the dead? A dead priest at that? This don't feel right," Hank's protest was fueled more by fear of divine retribution than sincere guilt.

"Nothing's felt right for a long time, kid," the old man said matter-of-factly, as he made his way out of the tent.

The boy couldn't help but agree.

CHAPTER FOURTEEN

Emerald was a dirty weed of a town, growing into an ugly city. In no way, shape, or form did it live up to its name. *Shit-Brown* or *Sepia* would have been more fitting names for this home of water-starved crabgrass, cracked dirt roads, and dull, neutral-colored buildings. In fact, the only thing that might warrant giving the dreary town of Emerald such a name was a mile or two outside of the town proper—*The Emerald Flower.*

The Emerald Flower was a three-story structure with a heavy French influence in the architecture. The windows were large, open arches with crudely carved cherry trim set against a green, painted facade. Each window led to iron-railed balconies on the second and third floors. Women, some beautiful and many others not so beautiful, smoked and leaned against the iron railings dressed in next to nothing.

In the context of Paris or New York, the building itself and the women within would have surely seemed cheap and run down. Here, in the middle of California, a mile away from the trading-post-turned-town of Emerald, The Flower stood out like an oasis of beauty and class.

Emmett dismounted his horse. He'd paid good money to rent a proper horse more suited for his size and weight than his old mule. He tied its reins to the post set up by a trough outside the bordello. He patted the animal absentmindedly as he took in the overwhelming visuals before him. A full day of riding, well into the night, had left him tired while approaching Emerald. Now in the nocturnal glow of the Flower, Emmett felt all fatigue vanish.

Emmett was no virgin. He was a strong, good looking young man, and as such had worked his way beneath the dress of a few girls back home. But they had been *girls*. What Emmett saw before him was the exposed, curvy flesh of full-grown *women*. They were like angels with broken wings, he thought. Their bodies soft, and white, and so beautifully proportioned. Their lacquered nails and red lips made them seem more than human. But their eyes, Emmett could see even from ten yards away, were empty and dark.

Like broken angels, he thought again. Perfect, seductive, divinely crafted bodies, devoid of spirit and cut off from the eternal. There was one in this building who, word had it, knew well the voice of the gods. Emmett came to The Emerald Flower to find her and her alone. Despite that intent, his young loins were now being called by these dead-eyed sirens. His mind, so set on the goal of opening the way to those places beyond, was being hijacked by the carnal instincts of his animal body.

Of course there would be a test, he thought. What man of great power, what sorcerer or spiritualist, has attained his potential without pushing back his baser self? He had already killed two men, stood at Hell's throne, and looked the beast called Nibelung in the eye. Surely he could resist the charms of a few whores.

Emmett approached the short staircase that led to the porch of the Flower. To the left of the door a heavy woman with heavy bosoms sat on a large, ugly man's lap as the two shared a bottle of wine. The ugly bastard's eyes were glued to her tits, but Emmett could not help but notice that her eyes, accompanied by a predatory smile, followed Emmett to the brothel's door. Equally uncomfortable and excited by this, Emmett awkwardly tipped his hat at the woman before entering the whorehouse.

The inside of The Emerald Flower was as impressive in its grandeur to Emmett as its exterior had been. The brothel was crowded on this night. Beauty was in abundance, both in flesh and atmosphere. The light was dim but comfortable. Oil lamps cast a soothing yellow glow across the large open foyer. Women with long flowing curls of hair and ample cleavage, pressed high up by corsets, laughed while sitting upon couches upholstered with soft, richly colored fabric. Wooden trim, carved with flowers and *fleur de lis* patterns, adorned every door and window. Carpeted staircases with iron rails ascended to upper floors where sounds of passion echoed forth.

Emmett stood in the doorway, dumbstruck and overwhelmed. The chemicals in his teenage body overtook his mind, filling him with the instinct to bed each and every woman in the room.

A hand reached out and gently squeezed Emmett's arm. He turned with a start, not because the sensation was unpleasant, but because he had been so absorbed by the carnal sights before him and subconsciously taken by the smell of sex that he had not noticed the woman who'd come to stand next to him.

"Pardon, sir. I didn't mean to startle you." The woman's voice was sultry and gravelly.

Emmett tipped his hat to the petite brunette woman before him, still uncomfortable. She was naked, save for a pair of stockings, and her simple proximity brought blood rushing to his manhood. He was a murderer twice over, and had seen dark things that no man was meant to, but he was still a sixteen-year-old boy surrounded by women of the night. As such, his nervousness was in equal measure to his excitement.

"Howdy, ma'am," Emmett stammered.

The whore smiled and squeezed his bicep a bit more firmly. "Ma'am, huh? Well ain't you just polite."

Unsure how to respond, Emmett simply moved forward with what he had been meaning to say.

"I'm looking for a woman."

The small brunette giggled and cast him a seductive glance "Well, I reckon you came to the right place." She then pushed her body close against his and whispered into his ear. "And look how quickly luck has shined upon you."

Instinct kicked in. Emmett gripped the woman by her slender, naked waist as she pressed against him. The smell of her hair intoxicated him and the gentle touch of her breathy words on his ear sent euphoria through his body. A voice called out in his mind, that deep, guttural, mental growl that continued to haunt him. It was a more dull roar this time, muted by the prospect of carnal union, but it was persistent. The voice reminded him that he come to Emerald to surpass the simplicity of the flesh and to tap into the infinite.

With great force of will, Emmett gently pushed the brunette whore away.

"I'm looking for a *specific* woman. A lady by the name of Fiona."

The undaunted worker before him smiled and ran a red lacquered nail down Emmett's bare forearm.

"Oh you don't need Fiona. I can make you feel the same things for half the coin."

"I'm, uhh, I mean I came here for her *other* skills."

"You're too young and handsome to need Fiona's mumbo jumbo. Fortune telling's for fools and needy old men. What you need is some *real* magic."

"I'm sure you're quite skilled at your trade, Ma'am, and you are mighty fetching, but I came a long way to meet Miss Fiona."

"Fine, go waste your money. Third floor, second door on the left."

Emmett nodded his thanks to the brunette woman with the slim body and soft flesh. As he turned away and headed toward the iron railed staircase, the animal in him fought against his ethereal aspirations, urging him to take the woman at hand and forget his fool's quest. Emmett was deeply touched by the cold breath of those that lay outside, though, and even the promise of the most intense magic of the natural world—the magic of flesh within flesh and physical union—would not thaw the growing winter within his soul.

***

Emmett knocked at the door to Miss Fiona's room. The sound of his soft rapping was lost behind the beating of his own heart, so busy pumping testosterone and adrenaline through his body, and blood to his nether regions.

After a full minute, no response had come. Emmett knocked again, louder this time.

A few seconds later the door opened, revealing a sliver of the room inside. In the space between the door and the frame a chain was drawn tight, connecting one to the other. Beyond that chain was a woman, older than Emmett had expected, perhaps his mother's age. She was nonetheless beautiful. Her hair was blond to the point of whiteness, and her skin was as fair as the freshly fallen snow that Emmett had only known in his nightmares. Her features were symmetrical and pleasing, elevated by a wide, crimson smile that revealed a full set of straight, ivory teeth. The generous curves of her nude form were as pleasing to Emmett's eyes as her upturned nose and high cheekbones.

"I'm quite sorry young man, but I've already found a companion for the night," she purred like a mountain cat.

She licked her teeth, bit her lip and smiled as she closed the door. Emmett's reflexes were quick though, and he was able to slip his boot between the door and the jamb.

This evoked a sudden look of anger from the woman named Miss Fiona.

"You're frightfully close to being removed from this here house!"

The voice that was not his own bellowed within his mind, *"Show her Nibelung's gold."*

And so Emmett obeyed the voice and produced a shining disk of gold, inscribed with ancient runes that he could not read. He held it up, directly in Miss Fiona's line of sight.

"That change your mind?" Emmett asked.

Fiona's expression was incredulous and angry. "You think you're the only man in here with money to spend?"

"I'd ask you to take a closer look, Ma'am," Emmett's tone was calm and respectful, but also firm.

Fiona gave the young man a questioning glance, than placed her attention on the Nibelung coin. At first she seemed not to recognize it, but seconds later something clicked. Her expression showed dawning recognition as she studied the arcane symbols emblazoned in the gold.

"Come on. I'm paying by the hour here," a gruff voice yelled from somewhere within the room. Fiona ignored the complaint and reached to touch the coin. Emmett nodded his consent and allowed her to take it from his hand. She then studied it, a childlike amazement in her eyes.

"Come on, whore! My cock ain't gonna suck itself!" complained the gruff voice again, this time with more anger.

Without a word, Fiona slammed the door shut. Before Emmett could attain a proper level of anger, he heard the jingle of the chain lock. A moment later the door opened wide, revealing the fully naked form of Miss Fiona, as well as the naked teamster in her lavish den.

Emmett entered with a sense of caution. Fiona turned from him, still studying the coin and walked deeper into her room.

"Get out," she said to the naked, gruff man who lay in her bed complaining. Her tone was absolute.

The man, fueled by anger and frustration sat up in the bed. "What? I paid you good money for that cooze and I intend to have my way."

"Remove him, please," the witch craned her neck and spoke the words back over her shoulder, in Emmett's direction.

Emmett did not respond verbally, but he did approach the bed, noting that he was stronger, younger, and larger than the angry man before him.

"Last chance to walk out on your own," Emmett spoke the words matter-of-factly, with an eerie detachment.

The older man, naked and intimidated by the large young man before him grabbed his clothes and got out of the bed. He grumbled as he did so, but made sure to give Emmett a wide berth. Once he was on his feet, the man made his way straight for the door, clothes in his arms. He dared not take the time to get dressed while still in the giant teenager's presence. Once the man was on the other side of the threshold, Fiona made a subtle gesture with the fingers of her left hand. The door slammed shut, seemingly of its own accord.

The beautiful, naked witch of fair skin and fair hair took her gaze away from Nibelung's gold and turned her attention to Emmett.

"Where did you get this?!" Her tone was not accusatory, but filled with excited curiosity.

"From a wretched creature who resides in the realm of death. Keep it. I have quite a bit more."

Fiona curled her fingertips around Emmett's and strode backward, leading him to her bed. She bade him to sit, and he did. Once Emmett was seated on her blood-red sheets, Fiona turned away from him and opened a drawer near her nightstand. She drew from within a small bowl, made from a black, mirrored stone that Emmett could not identify.

"What's that?" Emmett asked as Fiona got into a cross-legged sitting position on the bed, and placed the bowl between them.

"The stone is obsidian. I assume you didn't come here for a night of pirooting. This is the tool of my calling."

"I haven't said yet why I'm here."

"You obviously have a question that requires the skill of a seer to answer. I reckon you'd otherwise be hip-deep in me already."

"I won't lie, the thought crossed my mind."

"Of course it did. But we have more important matters, don't we? Ask me your question."

"How do I open the gate to those realms beyond death and Hell? Where do I find the path to eternity? How do I claim that power that taunts and beckons me?"

Fiona guided Emmett's hand to the rim of the black, mirrored bowl. "Keep those questions in your mind," she said as she pressed Emmett's hand against the razor edge of the obsidian bowl. The rim was so sharp that Emmett did not feel the cut at first, but only saw his blood pour into the basin. The dark red life that flowed from his palm looked black against the polished, pitch interior of the bowl.

After a small pool of the young man's blood had formed at the base of the bowl, Fiona traced the rim of the bowl with her own fingertips, cutting into them deeply. The blood that dripped from her fingers had the same black appearance within the bowl as Emmett's had. Unlike with Emmett, who now had a red blood welling up in his palm, Fiona's cuts leaked out a viscous, black fluid.

In the base of the bowl, Emmett's blood danced with the midnight sludge that had oozed out of Fiona. The two liquids repelled each other like oil and water, moving, changing shape within the basin. Fiona gazed into the bowl, watching the shapes like an owl following a mouse at night.

"He calls to you," she said. "Even now," Her voice was full of surprise and childlike wonder.

"Who?" Emmett asked, knowing full well that she spoke of the other voice that would occasionally growl in his mind.

The blood and ichor in the bowl moved about violently, only discernible by texture in the pitch-black vessel. The sludge from Fiona's veins formed a thick, lumpy background, while Emmett's blood took on a shape that looked like an angular letter "P" with the vertical line extending too far up.

"Thurs."

Emmett's heart froze for the space of three beats at the mention of the name. His insides went cold, as if someone had cut open his viscera and pumped in the waters of the February Atlantic.

"He is first amongst the devouring gods what lie past the veil. If the devil were real, he would tremble and piss in the shadow of Thurs." Fiona's words were reverent and sincere.

"Why does he call to me? Of all people?"

"You are a man of two worlds, cast aside by both," she said, gazing into the blue eyes that contrasted against his dark skin. "He is the creator of the earth and heavens, cast into the depths of a non-world."

Emmett followed her eyes as they returned to her scrying vessel. The mixture swirled into images that seemed meaningless to Emmett, but from which Fiona was capable of divining answers.

"You are a son, abandoned by your father. Thurs is the father of all, abandoned by his children."

"My father didn't abandon me," Emmett insisted, his voice quiet but defensive.

"Oh?" Fiona questioned. "Didn't he?"

Emmett ignored the accusation and shook his head.

"Again, why would something so powerful, the king of the gods or whatever, choose me?"

"Perhaps he finds you familiar. Perhaps it is luck. My advice is to thank the stars for your good fortune."

"And what does he want?"

"The same things you want. To cross the veil and sup upon the power of another world."

Fiona moved her scrying bowl to the nightstand by her bed, careful not to spill its contents. She then turned back toward Emmett, crawling across the bed on her hands and knees. Her movements displayed a grace that was feline and primal. Her smile was rife with predatory hunger.

"The gate between our world and that place beyond death can only be opened from this side of things. Do you want to open that gate? Do you dare?"

"I do. Want, that is, as well as dare."

Fiona placed one hand against Emmett's chest and pushed him back onto the soft, sanguine sheets. He went down with no resistance and allowed Fiona to crawl forward and straddle him. Her hair fell in his face, smelling of roses and cinnamon. Her flesh, so soft and smooth, grazed his own. Her already damp cunt pressed against the hardness in his denim jeans.

"I can show you the way to other worlds. I know the secret paths and I know the magic keys." An ear to ear grin—a maniac smile—stretched across her face. "But you must lie with me first."

Her hands reached down and tugged at Emmett's belt buckle. As soon as it loosened, she stopped and locked eyes with him, still grinning like a lunatic child.

"I would be most happy to oblige you on that front," Emmett said, his teenage heart beating like a war drum in his chest.

Without another word Fiona pulled at Emmett's pants. He lifted his ass off the bed, making her job easier. Once his hard cock was exposed she lowered herself upon him, not taking the time to fully undress him. Her thighs moved her body up and down, working his hardness in and out of her. Emmett closed his eyes and sighed in ecstasy as the warmth and wetness of her sex brought him euphoria.

Then he opened his eyes and nearly lost his mind.

The seer of The Emerald Flower's snow-white skin was now riddled with black veins that crisscrossed her flesh. The black, spider-web veins were everywhere, from her pock-marked thighs, to her sagging and shapeless breasts, to the wrinkles around her bloodshot eyes. Her chapped lips opened in a show of carnal pleasure, revealing broken, rotted teeth and a tongue as white as her skin.

Emmett tried to push the witch off of him, his strong hands grabbing her emaciated hips by the jutting pelvic bones. She hissed at his protest and brought a jagged, broken fingernail to rest an inch from his eye.

"You want to cross the bridge, you best pay the toll." Her voice held no more of the soothing sultriness of before. Now it was the voice of a throat riddled with cancer.

Emmett looked up at the vile thing that he had taken upon him and felt bile rise in his throat. Other thoughts fought for equal say in his mind—thoughts of the power he'd already gained—the ability to summon wealth and to trade one life for another—thoughts of what power, utterly alien to mankind, could still be tapped. He thought of his father, so strong, and smart, and perfect, and how he could honor him by surpassing him, if only in this way.

With a deep swallow, Emmett choked back the bile. His hands gripped the witch's bony hips and pulled her back onto him, until he was all the way inside her. Black, viscous liquid ran from her lady parts, forming a chunky, clotted pool on his pelvis. Emmett could feel the vile ichor working its way into his pisshole and burning his insides. Despite the pain and disgust, the boy raised his hips, driving himself hard within her.

"Show me the path, Fiona. Help me open the gate."

She let out a sound somewhere between a cackle and moan as she dug her broken nails into his hips.

"Thurs be praised!"

CHAPTER FIFTEEN

Time wasn't on the old man's side. Time was a primordial thing. Time was Kronus eating his children. Time was a Devourer, perhaps the most terrible of the whole lot. Time was the enemy.

Still, there were things to be done before he could face Thurs. To be ill-prepared would spell failure. The old man was all done with failure.

The priest's journal and train tickets had pointed the old man to where his war would end. An entry in the journal, scrawled with a shaky hand that was either terrified, drunk, or both recalled an up-and-coming town led by a raven-haired giant who could sway men's minds and darken their souls. His name was Mr. Thirsty, so called because of the cracked, dry look of his flesh.

Within the course of a few months the town had transformed itself, under the guidance of Mr. Thirsty, from an end-of-track shithole into a thriving village.

The journal was written in a broken narrative that mirrored fresh fear. Such a disjointed account would have struck the uninitiated as either the ravings of a mad man or shorthand notes penned by some dime novel author. Enough shared experience was held within the words for the old man to distill at least a vague sense of what the priest had seen.

Winter's End. That was the name of the eastern Nebraska town where Thurs had built his lair—a place where "*beneath the veil of normality the sinister lurks in every aspect,*" or so the priest had claimed.

Winter's End. This was the name of the place where the old man would fight his last battle.

It had been only hours since the old man and Hank had left Tanner's grove, and now the train was slowing to make its stop two hundred miles away at Winter's End. The old man wasn't ready for Thurs and had no intention of making his stand just yet. For now, they'd just wait on the train, and pass right through the enemy lines and onward to Omaha. If they were lucky enough not to draw the attention of Mr. Thirsty, that is.

Hank grimaced at the screech of the locomotive's brakes and the blare of its whistle. It was loud and ugly, bringing discomfort to his young, sensitive ears. It was a small price to pay for the experience of riding in a real train. Most folks who'd been born and raised in America had never been privy to such an experience. To see the world speed by you, to glide across the plains and through tunnels of bedrock—this was the magic of man. To hell with writhing, wooden messiahs and the secret rites of stone age shamans. The old man had shown Hank true power and beauty. The simple grace of a pistol. The red-hot rage of a steam engine.

The past held only death and darkness. Hank felt liberated from it. From here on out he was a child of today, and believer in tomorrow. If tomorrow was going to be reached, he knew he'd have to help the old man destroy the evil things that wanted to take the world back to yesterday.

The train slowed, halted, and rocked back a bit before coming to a complete stop. The old man looked out the window, over the town of Winter's End. He half expected a mob of witches or Thurs himself to be waiting at the station. This was not the case.

Townsfolk went about their business, up and down the dirt roads lined with storefronts, workshops, and homes. Folks got off the train, and a few got on. Businessmen and traders mostly, none bearing outward signs of witchcraft or madness.

Still, something about the place felt queer. To Hank, it was simply an odd feeling in his gut—an animal instinct that something just wasn't right. The old man was able to consciously pick up on the cracks within the facade. The *thorn* rune that took the place of the "p" on the swinging sign above the entrance to Patton's saloon. The smell of rain despite an open blue sky. The geometry and angles of the streets, designed for energy flow rather than ease of travel or economy of space.

And then there was the centerpiece. Right in the middle of town, about five hundred yards from the train depot, was the church. It seemed a simple and humble thing at first glance. Adobe construction, in the southwest style, only two stories in height. Its dusty, terracotta tone blended in with the earth below, and on top sat a simple whitewashed cross of wood.

Most travelers didn't give the church a second glance, and if they did, those folks would find themselves victim of nausea and vertigo. The great bulk of people who succumbed to these spells never gave it much thought. The old man knew the reasons for those sick feelings though.

He forced himself to study the lines of the building, willing out the vertigo as his mind tried to comprehend the impossible angles and spatial paradox of the architecture. The chaos was subtle, but it was there. Setting eyes upon the building was like viewing the world through shards of stray glass. One's mind can compensate and complete the picture of what it should be, but the truth of one's senses is a hideous image out of touch with reality.

For the space of five minutes the locomotive sat idle at the depot in Winter's End. During that span of time the old man barely breathed, anxiety crushing his chest like a weight. Part of it was the disorienting effect of the church. A bigger contributor to his anxious mindset was the knowledge that within that within the walls of that alien temple, just a few hundred yards away, his son was being held by a dark titan. There was another reason for his breathlessness as well, and a shameful reason at that. The old man was afraid of Thurs.

Hank lowered his head, rubbing his eyes as if he were weary.

"There's something weird about this place. It makes me dizzy."

The old man replied in a whisper, without looking over at his companion. "This is the place."

"So why are we still on the train?" Hank asked, darting up.

The old man placed a hand on Hank's shoulder, still keeping his eyes set on the church of impossible architecture.

"First things first. We got errands to run. Things to settle."

Hank said nothing, only looked back out the window, trying not to set his eyes on anything that made him feel dizzy. When the train began its slow crawl out of the depot, Hank was relieved. He'd had enough of Winter's End for the moment.

While the old man wasn't exactly relieved, his anxiousness did subside as the train left the damned town behind. He used to fear that when the time came he'd lose himself to rage and charge blindly at Thurs. It would seem that the final showdown would take a greater summoning of courage than he'd anticipated. On the positive side, at least fear would keep him grounded and focused. If it wasn't for the fear, the old man doubted his willpower would have been enough to keep him on road to Omaha so he could prepare.

**

The sun was low in the sky, and the blue canopy that had covered Winter's End had shifted color to a yellowish orange by the time the old man and Hank pulled into Omaha. Omaha was a fine city, in the old man's opinion, founded upon the proper principles of honest trade and human advancement. It embraced the future and held a vested interest in the continental railroad. It was a testament to what the will of man could accomplish, not thanks to any gods, but in spite of them. A bit too congested for his taste, but a fine place to rest with Hank and eat what might be his last meal.

The first stop was a modest wooden building with a simple whitewashed sign that read "Guns." The old man had ruined the business end of his best pistol back in his earthen prison months back. If he tried to shoot it now, the aim would be off at best. At worst, the barrel would explode.

"We getting a gun for me?" Hank asked with an excited smile.

"What the hell do you need a gun for?" the old man replied.

"Killing witches."

The old man grunted, sad that the boy had been exposed to the terrible things that lust for man's world. Part of him was a bit proud of Hank though. After what the boy had been through, it was amazing that he hadn't succumbed to insanity or constant fear. Instead he swallowed down the fear and was ready to fight.

He's a good soldier, the old man thought, as he messed up the boy's overgrown hair.

The door, a heavy beast of an entrance, was made up of thick planks of oak banded together with railroad ties. Hank tried to push it open, with all his might. He grunted, closing his eyes as he pushed with his legs. A few seconds later the door began to give. Hank didn't notice the old man's hand above him, taking the lion's share of the burden from him.

Inside the shop was dark, lit only by the fleeting rays of the setting sun as they came through the barred windows and open door. The space was small, but neat and well organized. Several rifles adorned the wall behind the register and old humidors on the counter were retrofitted into trays for ammunition.

The sole proprietor was a young man, probably still in his twenties. A series of nasty scars left one side of the gunsmith's face badly disfigured. The old man's best guess was some sort of shrapnel wound. The kid had been in the war, or at least the old man reckoned so.

"Howdy," the old man said in as friendly a voice as he could muster. "I could use a repair on my barrel."

The smith regarded the old man coolly, not yet saying anything.

Taking special care to use slow, deliberate movements so as not to alarm the scar-faced clerk, the old man pulled his pistol, *Donner*. He eyed it with appreciation for a moment. He was uncomfortable giving it up, even for the night. It was a simple repair though, not one that required his personal touch, and he had other affairs to see to.

After he placed the pistol on the counter, the clerk examined the gun with solemn appreciation.

"A Colt Dragoon?"

"Modeled after it, but not quite. A custom piece."

For a moment the gunsmith nodded his approval, as he turned the gun over in his hands, looking it over like he would a beautiful woman. As his eyes came to the barrel's end a bitter expression overtook his face.

"Whatcha do to this here iron? Drag it a mile 'cross granite?"

"That's closer to the truth than I care to admit," the old man answered. "Can you fix it?"

"If you got the money, yeah. Give me 'til tomorrow. Mid-morning."

Hank, while the old man and the clerk were talking, had taken to admiring the various firearms. Maybe it was mankind's natural love affair with things that kill, maybe it was that the old man's admiration for guns had become contagious, but Hank was enamored with collection of weapons that were for sale.

"Come on," the old man said, and motioned for Hank to follow him. The boy reluctantly turned away from the Winston repeater he was eyeing and followed the old man back out into the coming night. Once outside Hank turned toward the old man, with a serious expression on his young face.

"How am I supposed to help you kill this Thurs thing without a piece? You told me that only bullets can kill the Devourers."

"Come on," the old man repeated, ignoring both the boy's question and the unpleasant task that lay shortly ahead. "The train passed by a curio shop on the way here. Gonna give her a look."

"What's a *curious* shop?"

"*Curio,*" the old man corrected. "A shop that sells unusual odds and ends. Taxidermied animals, antique junk, old books."

"Why we going there?"

"Every once in a while the charlatans that run these places stumble upon a bit of real magic—bones from monsters, black bibles, cursed weapons."

"I thought powder and flint held all the magic we needed?"

"Yes. But if we found something of an arcane nature, we could glean more into the mind of the enemy. We could also acquire said damnable things and destroy 'em. Cut down the enemy's arsenal a bit."

Hank nodded in understanding and the two walked in silence for ten minutes or so. It wasn't an awkward quiet, but rather a silent peace that comes about when folks are truly comfortable around one another.

The curio shop was little more than a tin-roofed shack surrounded by tacky statues and various pieces of Americana. Once it was in sight the old man turned toward Hank with an expression that nearly gave hint of a smile.

"Plus, curios just have some interesting shit. Kind of fun to look around."

Fun. The concept seemed as alien to the old man as the word sounded coming from his mouth. The strangeness of it—this grizzled, vengeance fueled, old-as-dirt warrior suggesting something fun—caused Hank to smile.

A piece of poultry wire nailed to a few rotted boards served as the front door. The old man pulled it open, allowing Hank to enter first. The inside was dim, lit by several small candles that did little to combat the oncoming darkness of night. They weren't meant to though. Rather, the old man suspected, the dancing flames were there to cast suspicious shadows on to the tightly packed knick-knacks for sale. Smoke and mirrors, to transform mundane refuse into treasured mysteries.

The parlor trick salesmanship was winning Hank over with a quickness, just as the old man reckoned it would. The boy was bouncing from treasure to treasure. One moment a grainy photograph of the Great Sphynx would captivate him, then a pyrite necklace would glitter in the corner of his eye and demand his attention. The old man was amused. It was a feeling he hadn't felt in years.

Hank's excitement did not go unnoticed by the shop keep either. The proprietor, who was a gangly old thing with the demeanor of carnival worker, watched him with deep interest. The old man reckoned this was partially to make sure the little bastard didn't steal anything, partially because he suspected it would be an easy feat to relieve the boy of any money he might have.

The old man tipped his hat at the shop keep but didn't speak. The shop keep gave the old man a nod in return, then shot his gaze back upon the boy who was now admiring a geode about the size of a robin's egg.

The old man gave the tiny shop a quick scan, looking for anything that might relate to witchcraft. To his relief there was nothing.

"Come take a look at this!" Hank cried.

The old man walked over, trying not to knock down anything in the space that could barely contain his height and girth. He found Hank gawking at a queer taxidermied spider, the size of the old man's fist. Bright orange dominated its exoskeleton, which looked to have turned soft and spongy by whatever chemicals preserved it. White tendrils shot out from its limbs and from one of its mandibles. It almost appeared to be half plant.

"Ever seen something so crazy looking?!" Hank exclaimed in excitement and disgust.

"It ranks up there, I'll give you that."

The old man nonchalantly reached for his remaining pistol as soft footfalls came up behind him. Instead of an attack came a voice. The old man relaxed his hand as the shop keeper spoke.

"That right there may be the strangest piece I've ever come across," the garbage slinger said, beginning his sales pitch. "You may think you know what that is, but I bet ya beer money that you are wrong." He spoke in a voice that was creaky and rough, like cracking wood set against unoiled hinges.

"It's a spider," Hank replied.

"And you'd be owing me a beer, young 'un. That ain't a spider at all."

"Sure looks like a spider," the old man chimed in.

"Sure as shit does, I agree. But it ain't."

The shop keeper reached for Hank's hand, and placed the boy's fingers gently against the spider. It felt soft and porous, not at all like a spider had any right to feel.

"Ewww"

"See?" the shop keep croaked. "Ain't no spider. Least not anymore."

"What is it then?" Hank asked.

"A fungus, like mushrooms, but a special kind of fungus. A parasitic Fungus."

"What's that mean?"

"Means that once upon a time, this poor bastard was a regular old spider, eating bugs and birds, humping on lady spiders, doing normal ole spider things. Then somewhere along the line this fungus got in its blood, and started taking it over like. Replaced his flesh and blood and other spider bits with its own stuff. Eventually Mr. Spider here kicked the bucket, but the fungus kept on eating away at his body, and growing in his place. Now there ain't nothing left of Mr. Spider but a mushroomy shadow."

Hank pulled his hand back and shook it wildly.

"Shit! Did I get it in me?"

A disquieting laugh creaked out from the shop keep's throat.

"No worries, boy. The fungus been dead quite a spell too. Ain't no danger."

The old man had turned away from the two of them suddenly and headed for the door. A pair of stray tears ran down his face. He didn't know what had brought about the crying, nor did he care to get introspective.

"Where you going?" Hank asked, not wanting to leave the house of mysteries.

The old man did not turn around, but he did stop at the door. He pretended to rub the exhaustion from his eyes, and he buried down the pain that was physically erupting from him.

"I need some fresh air."

Before walking out the door, the old man placed a greenback on the counter.

"Buy yourself something fun, Hank."

With that he walked out the door and looked up toward the hated stars.

I'm coming for you tomorrow, the old man projected the thought upward. The stars did not respond.

***

Hank walked out of the curio shop, having purchased a pendant of driftwood carved into the shape of a raven. He saw good luck in the pendant's graceful form.

"You remember the ravens up in the mountains?" Hank asked the old man, who was smoking a cigarette outside.

"Yep. I'd say we owe them a debt. Might not have gotten my hand on my pistol if they hadn't of pissed off that lunatic."

"I figure as much too. That's why I picked this." Hank showed off the wooden raven as he spoke.

"That's a fine choice, Hank."

The old man reached down and took the pendant between his thumb and forefinger, admiring the simple beauty of its craftsmanship.

"My own pa was as taken up with myth as much as my wife. A whole different set of stories, but the same kind of nonsense. As a kid I loved hearing his stories about the gods and heroes of the old country. 'Course those stories were silliness at best, but when that maniac started cursing about them 'crows,' my pa's nonsense came to mind and I found a bit of wisdom in it."

"Yeah?" Hank asked.

"See, the king of the gods was a tough, slippery, old bastard. He had to be that way, because his enemies were worse. But he had these two pet ravens that acted as his eyes across the world. In English their names would have been *Thought* and *Memory*."

"There were two ravens outside the cabin!" Hank exclaimed, eager to latch on to any belief the old man might have.

"Well that's just coincidence, but it got me thinking. Sometimes the world makes a bastard of ya. Chance and circumstance can turn the kindest man into a murderer, or a thief, or both faster than anyone would care to admit. But what keeps you human, what guides you home, is thought and memory."

The old man paused before asking Hank if he understood.

"I think," Hank replied.

"Thought—critical, logical thought—that's what separates a man from an animal. That's what keeps us progressing further and further. That ability to think our way around any and every problem is why the Devourers fear us."

"And what about memory?" Hank asked.

"Memory is what keeps us strong in the toughest times, and it's what prevents us from becoming monsters when our hands are forced to kill. It's the memories of love and happiness that let us come home from the dark places where the world sometimes takes us. It's memory that lets a man find the strength to fight the gods themselves for what's right."

Hank hung his head down in shame and said, "I try not to remember most of the time".

"I understand," the old man said between drags of his cigarette.

"I miss them so much," Hank muttered, trying to suppress a sob.

"Tell me something good about your folks. Something from when life was at its best."

"You first," Hank replied with tears in his eyes. He didn't think he was ready to revisit those happy moments just yet. He was sure that the single-minded witch killer wouldn't have it in him to share about his family.

The old man called his bluff. He recounted the way his wife would tell these ludicrous Indian myths as if they were fact, and how he was always torn by his hatred for superstition and how beautiful she sounded when she told them.

He laughed, actually *laughed*, taking about his son imitating him, pretending to shave by slathering his face with soap and scraping it away with a fork.

Hank, seeing actual happiness in the old man's face, gave in and told his own stories. He talked about how proud his folks had been on the day when they walked away from the plantation to forge their own path. He recalled with misty eyes the sound of his parents' voices belting out gospels in perfect harmony.

For the rest of the evening, the old man and his young friend wandered the quiet, dark streets of Omaha, smoking rope and trading fond stories of their lost loved ones.

For the first time since they'd met, the old man didn't look so old to Hank. The boy began to think that the poor guy was a mite younger than first impressions would suggest.

Late into the night, Hank began to waver, clearly losing his battle against exhaustion. The old man picked the boy up in his strong arms, and carried him until he was sound asleep.

Once Hank was out cold, the old man headed over into the poorest section of town he could find, the part of town where he figured the Negroes lived. He walked unrushed, taking comfort in the warm sensation of holding the boy in his arms, and looked for a home that showed signs of children. Eventually he stopped at tiny hovel where a crude, wooden doll with straw hair lay by the door.

It was nearly three in the morning by this point, but the old man knocked on the door anyway. After a minute or so, a scared-looking black man, maybe in his early twenties, opened the door. The sight of the enormous Confederate warrior sent a tremble of terror through the man's body. Word was getting around about a so-called knighthood of Confederates who were lynching blacks, and here was a gray-coated monster holding a black child in his arms.

The old man only said "Shhh," as he pushed past the terrified occupant of the house. The place was really just two rooms. This first room held two mattresses. On one lay a sleeping little girl with ebony skin. She was maybe three or four years old, the old man reckoned. On the other mattress lay a woman, who was presumably the girl's mother. She was awake and filled with an even greater depth of fear than her mate who had answered the door.

The old man walked over to the latter mattress and gently lay the boy on the bed, careful not to wake him. On the floor near the mattress he dropped a small pack that contained the few belongings Hank had acquired since they left the Sierra Nevada—a few scraps of his parents' clothes, and random rocks and sticks that had caught his fancy. The old man had also slipped his own backup pistol into the pack. It was a tough world, and the boy might need a piece from time to time.

The old man turned back toward the door and stepped uncomfortably close to the trembling man of the house. The old man locked gaze with the man, meaning to invoke his fear.

He let his own pack slip down his shoulder and to his hand, then reached in. The old man was sizing up the man at the door, trying to gauge his character. Fear was visibly written across his face, and he was rapidly swallowing spit and terror. Still, he didn't turn away, and that was something.

He'll do all right, the old man decided.

Instead of drawing a pistol or a knife from the pack, the old man pulled out a fistful of greenbacks. He pushed them into the man's chest, still locking his gaze.

"You take care of this boy. You do him right, as if he was your own."

The old man got closer this time and hunched down to bring himself level with the other man, leaving only fractions of an inch between their noses.

"I'll be checking up. Making sure he's treated well."

Without another word, the old man exited the hovel and left the terrified, confused family to ponder what had just happened.

CHAPTER SIXTEEN

The air was dry and hot on the morning when Emmett finally rode back into town and up to his house. The parched ground beneath his feet was cracked and broken, just like the rashy, dry flesh of his body. The summer air and the unforgiving sun exasperated Emmett's discomfort, but he had managed to compartmentalize the irritation and focus on the enlightenment that had so recently elevated his mind and spirit.

No one had been in the streets as Emmett rode through the center and all the shops were closed up. He guessed that would make it Sunday and put most folks at church. The concept of time had confounded him while within the warm embrace of The Emerald Flower. Minutes had expanded to the space of hours and days had compressed into seconds. Truthfully, Emmett could not even guess as to how long he'd been away.

It had not been just inside the whorehouse that Emmett had experienced this time dilation. On his ride home, this strange, shifting perception continued. Rattlesnakes had issued slow-motion warnings to his horse, taking a full minute to swing their tails back and forth a single time. Maggots writhing within the carcass of some fallen rodent lived out their life cycle, transforming into flies and dying of old age within the blink an eye.

These insane sensations had lessened in severity the further on he rode. Only now, just outside of town, had things really begun to feel normal again. Emmett was unsure if this was the truth though. Had reality calmed itself and settled back into the shape he had known since birth, or had he simply grown accustomed to this new vision of the world, like a man wearing spectacles recovers from the initial dizziness they cause?

Emmett patted his horse on the side and tied him to the fence that bordered his home. Surely his mother would ask where the animal had come from, but Emmett didn't care at the moment. His body was tired and pained. His mind was reeling with what he'd experienced since meeting Fiona, and the possibilities of experiences yet to come. The least of his concerns was placing his mother's mind at ease about a new horse.

Emmett walked with extra care down the dirt path from the log post fence to his front door. He was afraid that time might go wild and he would lose his footing, or that he might fall from exhaustion. Neither happened. His hand touched the front door and he smiled, glad to be home.

He pushed the door open and took in the happy scent of fresh baked bread and vegetable soup. His mother stood at the stove with her back to him, stirring a pot.

"Hi, Ma," Emmett spoke the words nonchalantly.

She turned around and cast a glance that reflected neither expression that Emmett had expected. There was no joyous relief that he was home, nor anger that he had been missing for who knows how long. Her eyes were bloodshot and brimming with tears, and a great sadness resonated throughout her entire face. Emmett had never seen such an expression on his mother, not when she was dying, nor when his father left for war. It broke his heart to look upon.

"Ma, what's wrong?"

Her lips trembled and tears broke forth from the dam of her will.

"You went and saw your grandfather, didn't you? You went and saw my bastard of a father!"

Emmett's mind reeled at the accusation. How could she have known? Had someone followed him? Had some Paiute son of a bitch come to town and run his mouth?

"Ma, I've been off picking up work. I ain't never met your pa. Never had the time nor the inclination to seek him out."

Now anger snuck its way into his mother's sorrowful expression. Her brown eyes lit up with fury behind the tears. Her trembling lips stiffened into a thin, straight line.

"No!" she yelled. "No, Emmett! You do not lie to your kin! Your pa and I taught you better than that."

"I'm not lying, Ma," Emmett lied, reaching out his hands in a gesture of faux sincerity.

His mother, anger still resonating through her body language but not overshadowing her sadness, reached into a small pocket of the apron she wore. A moment later she produced a silver coin. It was one of the Nibelung coins, covered with inscriptions of sharp, angular runes. The most prominent of them was the rune that he'd seen in the scrying vessel where his blood had danced with Fiona's ichor—that sharpened "p" shape that was too long at the top.

"Then what the hell is this, Emmett?" She screamed the words and threw the coin across the room at him. It bounced off of his chest and clattered harmlessly against the floor.

Emmett knelt down and picked up the coin, running his thumb across the inscriptions, which instinctively made more sense after his time in the witch's bed.

"It's silver. Some old coin from Europe, I reckon. Traded it for one of Pa's custom pistols."

"Do you think I'm a stupid woman, Emmett?" His mother shook her head in grief, anger, and disbelief.

"I'm a shaman's daughter. You think I don't recognize those symbols? You think my father, before he went mad, didn't warn me of the evil, hungry spirits who claw at the door to our world?"

Emmett turned his gaze down and stared at the symbol on the coin, the one he knew in his heart to be the crest of Thurs himself. It was no use lying. He had hurt his mother enough and he was too tired, both in mind and body, to continue the charade.

"Pa's not here," Emmett whispered, still looking down at the piece of silver in his hand.

"What?" Emmett's mother asked, completely thrown off by her son's statement.

"Pa's not here." This time Emmett raised his head and looked his mother in the eyes. "If he was, he'd have found way to save you. He'd have found a cure, or found a better doctor, or marched across the frozen wastes of Hell and shot Death herself in the face."

Emmett gulped and felt the urge to cry, but no tears came.

"Pa wasn't here, so I had to be the man. But I ain't as smart as him and I ain't able to will the world to my liking the way he can."

"Emmett ..." her voice had now softened and the anger was fleeing.

"I'm not him. I can't eyeball a rock's worth and smelt it into steel, then work the damn steel into a pistol. I can't see a machine in my mind, then will it into life with my hands and some tools. I can't see every angle of an impossible problem, and work out a miraculous solution."

Emmett's mother stared at him, dumbstruck with sorrow and pity. She was unable to speak.

"I'm not Pa and I couldn't beat that reaper. So I went to the only other man who I thought might have a chance."

"No, baby. Tell me you didn't do this for me!"

"Why? It worked!" Emmett was screaming now. "I took that magic, magic even your father feared, and I walked into Hell, and I saved your life!"

"But at what cost, baby? Nothing's free in this world, nor any other."

Emmett nodded and blinked.

"The cost? A life for a life. Blood for blood. And I'd pay it again in a heartbeat, Ma." His voice had gone from sad and insecure to righteous.

"That's why I'm better? You killed someone—killed some innocent person to save my life?"

She strode across the room and stopped before her son. Emmett was nearly a foot taller than his mother, and she looked up at him with a sad and angry glare.

"What gave you that right?" she asked, tears streaming down her face.

Emmett didn't answer. After a moment of silence between them, her brown eyes locked with his blue, and Emmett's mother smacked him across the face with all the strength she could muster.

"You're not God! You don't get to choose who lives and dies, Emmett!"

Emmett turned his gaze back to his mother, recovering from the open-hand strike to his cheek. There was no anger in his face, but rather an inkling of pride and amusement, of which Emmett himself wasn't fully aware.

"No, I'm not God, Ma. Not yet."

With that he walked around his mother and toward the stove.

As he walked away his mother spoke again. "You go pack your things. We're leaving town."

Without turning around, Emmett grabbed a bowl from the cupboard. The same bowl with Paiute symbols that had inspired his first steps down the dark path he'd taken. He found it interesting that the symbols looked nothing like the angular runes he had found in The Cavern of the First Breath.

"Don't be ridiculous, Ma. This is our home. Pa will make it back soon. Why would we leave?"

"Sheriff Silver knows, Emmett. He found blood in the shop, between the floorboards. He found that coin, and he might not know the symbols, but he knows they ain't right."

Emmett ladled vegetable soup into his bowl while he spoke back. "A little blood and an antique coin don't hold much weight. Could be animal blood. A stray coon got in the shop."

"What about Mackum's body. I didn't want to believe him, but he says someone choked him to death. Someone with hands bigger than he'd ever seen, except on you and your pa."

Emmett had pulled a spoon from the drawer as his mother spoke and was now slurping up the broth and some small peas that floated within it. It tasted delicious and his body greedily sucked up the nutrients. After taking three spoonfuls of the soup he finally spoke.

"Still no real proof. Just suspicion."

He took another spoonful of the rich broth.

"You think this is New York or Philadelphia, Emmett? This is Affirmation, California! There ain't no proper courts here. There's the law and one man to enforce it. He's gonna shoot you down or string you up if we don't leave town tonight!"

"And why would he warn my mother?"

"Out of respect for your pa. He said if I could get you to leave he'd forget about you, but if you stayed in his town, there'd be a funeral."

Emmett gave up on the spoon and drank down the rest of the soup straight from the bowl. Once he had downed the entire bowl he pulled out the handkerchief that hung from his back pocket and wiped his mouth.

"If he starts thinking you're more than a killer, if he starts thinking you're a witch, then things are gonna turn worse than a noose or a bullet."

"He'll find out," Emmett replied calmly and turned to face his mother. "And things will be much worse than a noose or a bullet."

With that being said, Emmett walked off to his bedroom and closed the door, leaving his mother crying in the kitchen. He fell into his bed and kicked off his boots. It felt good to take them off and even better to lie down. As peaceful sleep overtook him, Emmett could hear his mother crying in the other room. This saddened him, but he took comfort in the fact that he needn't lure a sacrifice to him to serve as a key this time. A sacrifice would come to him—a silver key to unlock infinity. All he had to do was sleep and wait.

***

Patrick Silver sat at his kitchen table and prayed for the first time in years. He spoke Hebrew words, words he could barely remember the meaning of, and hoped God might listen after such a long silence on his part. There was always a chance. Silver had never lost faith exactly, but he'd been preoccupied in the practical and material.

Another reason he hadn't been observant over the last few years was one he was more ashamed to admit. Silver was a Jew in a town with no others. Enough folks had issue with him over that as it was. No need to draw attention to it. If he could forget it, maybe they would too.

Of course they hadn't, at least not all of them. Pricks like Mackum liked to blame any crime that happened within twenty miles on the fact that a cowardly Jew was sheriff. Others would make comments and jokes on Sundays when he didn't go to church. But for the most part, people respected Patrick Silver and some even counted him amongst their friends.

Tonight Silver could care less if every last person in this damn town heard him pray in the language of his forebears. The truth was he needed God because he was more than a little afraid of Emmett Wongraven. The boy was a mountain of a man, just like his father. He was also a killer, that much Silver was sure of. But there was something worse. Emmett was into something dark, something that Silver couldn't fathom, despite all the "Jew secrets" that some folks thought he knew.

Silver put on his hat, a brown derby with a dark gray trim, and headed out his front door. Outside, the night seemed off. The moon was new and its light was absent from the sky. The only illumination came from far away stars, which seemed to spread their radiance in irregular, shifting patterns. Silver had never been much of a stargazer, but looking up into the infinite heavens on that night, he thought things looked mighty odd. He wasn't positive what stars should be where exactly, but he was pretty sure they were all in the wrong place.

The night was hot. Only a degree or two Fahrenheit had retreated beyond the horizon with the sun at dusk. Silver's heels clicked loudly on the parched earthen street, echoing through the still night like a giant's beating heart.

No one else roamed the streets on this late night. Partly because Monday morning, with all the demands it brought, was fast approaching. Silver was pleased with this small concession. If things went awry, there wouldn't be a bunch of mouth-breathing gawkers standing around to catch a stray slug.

The Wongraven house, a home where he'd had dinner on more than one occasion, was a fifteen-minute walk away from his own home. In the past he'd made the walk with a sense of cheerfulness. There hadn't been so much a sense of belonging amongst the gunsmith, his native wife, and their mixed-breed son. Rather, Silver had a comforting sense that he wasn't the only outsider living in Affirmation.

Like everyone else who spent any time around the gunsmith and his wife, Silver had grown to respect them greatly. The woman was as kind-hearted and beautiful as a man could ever have hoped to meet. Not a negative word nor a dribble of gossip ever escaped her lips. She was the best damn cook in town and a fairly talented seamstress.

What's more, she must have been diligent and skilled in her womanly duties, as the gunsmith, who strode through this ugly town like a Roman statue come to life, never seemed to return the flirtatious glances that more than few women would cast his way.

Emmett's father was a plain-spoken man who judged everyone and everything by their merit, rather than by their last name or their skin tone. He was a proper, gentile white man, who chose to take an Injun as his wife and befriend a Jew sheriff, and made no apologies. Silver admired that about Wongraven, but it also had a way of making him feel small. Here was a man who was admired, despite telling societal convention to fuck all. Meanwhile, Silver tried to underplay his heritage and still struggled for respect.

Maybe that right there was the difference. The gunsmith had gained respect because he acted in manner that demanded it. Respect for Silver mostly stopped at his badge, and maybe because he acted in way that was disrespectful to himself.

Or maybe everyone was just too scared to say shit to Wongraven, or even behind his back, seeing as the man was six foot six and could shoot a pimple off a fly's ass.

It was because of that respect that Patrick Silver was willing to give their son one chance to get the hell out of town. He'd known Emmett since he was a boy, but never had any strong feelings about him one way or another. He did worry about Emmett, though. He'd seen him struggle and get harassed by other kids over his black hair and olive skin—kids who didn't fear his father the way their parents did.

He'd also seen Emmett become aware of the size and strength he'd inherited from his old man. He recalled on time the boy pummeled three little shits who thought that together they might "break the savage."

Silver knew that the young man had reasons to be angry. The sheriff himself knew how hard anger could be to check. Ever since his dad went running off to fight for the Confederacy and his mom took ill, that anger in Emmett seemed to be burning like a wildfire. Maybe if he'd stepped in earlier and tried to talk with the boy, he could have helped him check that rage. Now it was too late. The boy had not just crossed the line, he had galloped over it like a stampeding horse.

Silver had hoped that the twelve weeks the boy had disappeared for would have turned into a thing of permanence. Word was that Emmett rode back into to town this morning though, looking like he'd crawled his way across the Mojave. Responsibility lay with the sheriff to eject this dangerous element, by persuasion, intimidation, or violence, if it came to it. Silver feared it would.

Twenty minutes after he'd left his front door, Silver found himself by the fence outside of the Wongraven home. From inside Silver heard the sound of deep, almost guttural moans. The terrible wailing was like that of a bear with its leg caught inside a trap.

Silver walked down the dirt path toward the front door, consciously softening his footfalls and placing his right hand on his iron. As he got within arm's reach of the door, he could hear a soft, choking sound beneath the monstrous wails. Part of him wanted to run. Part of him wanted to set fire to the place from the outside, and just burn away whatever horrors might lie inside. Missus Wongraven would surely be in there too though, and Patrick Silver just couldn't carry the weight of her death on his conscience.

He placed his left hand on the brass doorknob in front of him and fear caught in his throat, as if he'd swallowed an apple whole. The sheriff did not want to lay eyes upon source of the wretched, tormented sounds inside, whatever it was.

He muttered one final prayer, this one informal and spoken in English. He tightened his hold on the walnut grip of his pistol. With all the courage he could summon, the lawman turned the knob and pressed against it.

The door was unlocked and swung open easily. The moans and choked gurgling were louder now, pouring forth through the open doorway. Across the threshold, darkness reigned and Silver could not make out the sources of the sorrowful cacophony. The Sheriff cursed himself for not bringing matches. With his heart pounding in his chest, he stepped across the threshold and into the darkened home.

"Kylie?" Silver called out in a voice that he hoped sounded sure and strong.

CHAPTER SEVENTEEN

As luck would have it, there was an all-night saloon near the train depot in Omaha, a big, well-kept place that also served as a hotel. The old man had spent the past several hours nursing watered-down whiskeys. His thoughts were muddled, not from the cheap booze, but from lack of sleep and long suppressed emotions forcing their way to the forefront of his stubborn brain.

Through a nearby window he could see that the sun was well above the horizon. A massive steam engine sat against the clear blue horizon—a symbol of mankind's bright future. Part of his mind, a part that was as selfish as it was wise, screamed for him to forget the past and all the pain it held. The voice pleaded for him to bid farewell to his son, his wife, his war, and every other damn thing that urged him toward certain doom.

Start a new life, it begged. *Go get the boy and find a plot of land and live the rest of your life.*

But this voice was not his own, the old man concluded. This was the voice of Cowardice, another one of the Devourers. It was a voice born from the poison in his blood. He looked down at the bloated, black leech on his arm. The creature looked a mite more monstrous than any other leech he'd ever seen before.

It was time.

The old man settled his tab with the bartender and headed outside. He breathed in a deep lungful of air and found it only slightly tainted with the poisonous touch of burnt coal. The sun was warm against his skin. Folks were walking down the street, smiling as they went about the mundane business of their day. Birds, hidden within the boughs of trees, were singing love songs.

It was a good day to die.

There was a little less than an hour before the train heading west toward Winter's End would leave the station. This left the old man plenty of time to retrieve his pistol from the local gunsmith, who was not too far from the depot.

A bittersweet feeling had overcome the old man as he walked through the door to the gun shop. His journey was almost over, and with any luck his boy would soon be saved. He found himself sad at leaving Hank behind. What was to come at Winter's End was nothing that kid needed to see, though. At least here, in Omaha, he'd have a chance at some kind of life.

The smith was standing behind the counter, polishing the old man's prized pistol. The damaged barrel had been cut back just a hair, and was finished to look just like new.

"That's some fine work," the old man commented as he walked up to the counter.

The gunsmith didn't respond. In fact he seemed to not even notice the old man. His sole focus was the gun named Donner. In his eyes was a deep admiration—no, a burning obsession with the piece.

"Hello?" The old man called for the smith's attention. This time he turned around. He looked at the old man with a confused expression.

"You did my gun up right. What do I owe ya?" the old man asked.

Recognition came across the shop keep's face. He suddenly remembered the old man and realized why he was here.

"Your gun? I don't remember you dropping off no gun, you slaving bastard."

There was a deep hatred in the gunsmith's voice, and a madness in his eyes. Somehow Thurs had gotten to him. This wasn't some fool trying to steal from him. No, this was a desperate attempt to rob the old man of the weapon that would end the dark titan's contemptible existence.

"You ain't thinking right, son. Just hand me my gun and I'll hand you your pay. Everybody wins."

The old man knew from experience that he was as likely to talk down this man who had been touched by the Devourers as a deer was likely to persuade a mountain lion not to eat him. Despite this knowledge, the old man still had a dislike of killing, regardless of how much he'd done it. Now his hesitation would cost him.

The gunsmith took two swift steps back. The old man was unable to make up the distance quickly enough with the counter between them. The few seconds impediment that the counter imposed was just enough for the smith to raise Donner and fire off a round.

The lead slug tore through the old man's right shoulder, sending shockwaves of pain throughout his upper body. The force of the gunshot knocked him off of his feet.

The world spun around him. Phantom fireworks exploded in his field of vision. Spikes of fiery pain had their way with his nerves. Once his mind recovered enough to produce a conscious thought, all it could say was *not yet.*

A moment later the gunsmith appeared above the old man and trained the .44 straight down into his right eye.

"You walk around in that shitbag, gray jacket like your kind ain't got they asses whooped," the crazy eyed gunsmith growled. "Think you can start a war, maim and kill folks, and then we're all peaches and cream after you slink away in shame?"

The hammer clicked into place.

"Ain't no room in this world for Confederate ghosts."

The old man, who was not quite as old as he seemed, crossed his legs around the younger man's right calf. With surprising quickness he hooked his boot behind the smith's knee and jerked it forward. The shop keep stumbled to his knees. At the same time the old man forced his screaming nerves into submission and rolled toward the right, hoping to un-align himself with the trajectory of any oncoming bullet.

The .44 thundered and a slug found purchase within the rough wooden floor, about two inches from the old man's head. He didn't let that distract him any more than he had let the incredible pain in his shoulder distract him. With all the strength left in his shot-up, beaten, poisoned, and war-ravaged body, he kicked out and introduced the gunsmith's jaw to the hard leather of his boot. A sound like shattering porcelain escaped the smith's mouth. This sound was followed by a second, awful noise that was somewhere between a scream and a moan. The scar-faced man fell onto his side as blood poured from his mouth, carrying bits of shattered teeth like so much flotsam in its crimson current.

The pistol had fallen from the smith's hand and lay between them. With a slow determination, the old man sat up and reached for the gun. Since his opponent was fighting for consciousness the old man saw no reason to race for the firearm. He did, however, keep his eyes trained on the smith as he wrapped his leathery hands around the pistol's grip.

The blast of the .44 had left a ringing in the old man's ears and he did not hear the door open behind him. He was still sitting on his ass, unaware of anyone but the bleeding man in front of him, when he felt the cold steel of a gun barrel press against the back of his skull.

"Drop the iron, old man, and stand up nice and slow."

The old man took a moment to measure his options. With a slug in his arm, working on no sleep, and sitting flat on his ass, he could see no scenario in which fighting back could result in anything but the spraying of his gray.

The old man placed his gun on the ground. He then rose to his feet, which took a bit of effort, and placed his hands on the back of his head.

A well-built man with sandy blond hair and a mustache that was far too big for his face walked a wide arc around the old man, until they were face to face. The man, whose gun was trained on the old man, wore a copper sheriff's badge and a brown, wide-brimmed hat. There was something in the lawman's eyes, not the madness of a witch, but a touch of natural, human sadism. This was pretty common, the old man thought, in lawmen. There was also a keen intelligence behind those brown eyes. As a demonstration of that intelligence, the lawman didn't get too close to the old man. He kept the distance advantage that his iron gave him.

"Now drop that big ole pig sticker and any other weapons you might got."

"The man tried to cheat me. I was just taking what was mine."

Talking his way out of this was probably a long shot, but the old man held no other cards at the moment. If he put up a fight then he'd surely die before his appointment in Winter's End.

"Well now that you explained it," the lawman replied, still keeping the gun level on the old man's center mass, "I obviously believe the sword-wielding crazy who just kicked my good friend's teeth in."

The old man unhitched the sword from his back and let it drop without another word. He didn't let his eyes leave those of the lawman for even as a second as he did so. He needed to remember this face. This man was going to cost him a day at least, and if the coming detour were too cost him his son's life ... well, he wanted to be sure he would remember who'd caused the loss of another war.

The thought of the time that was escaping filled the old man with a deeper hate than he had experienced in all his hard life. In his mind's eye he could see Kronos laughing at him, as bits of the titan's children dripped down its chin. His heart and mind became a white hot furnace of rage, and in a man of smaller will, that anger would have grown into a wild fire. He kept it in check, but barely.

"We ain't had a good thief-hanging in a spell," the lawman said with a grin.

The old man said nothing, but hidden beneath his shirt the leech on his arm was growing larger by the second, sucking at the infected blood and the hatred within it.

***

A full day had gone by since the old man had been arrested for attempted murder and armed robbery. He'd been told that there'd be a hanging within a few days, and that he of course would be the belle of the ball. He supposed that trials for outsiders were a rarity in railroad cities like Omaha.

The bullet hole in his shoulder, right around the same place where the Indian had nailed him with the poison dart, ached something fierce. At least the slug had gone clear through, and the wound didn't feel infected. The sheriff had seen to it that a doctor came in and patched up the shoulder wound. Couldn't have him die before the gallows show.

The doctor had made note of the leech, and the black veins upon which it sucked, but made no moves to cut it away. The parasitic creature looked sick to him, and he wanted nothing to do with whatever infection it was feasting on. *A wise idea*, the old man had thought.

That was the day before, just a bit after he'd been tossed into his tiny cell in the Omaha jailhouse. The jailhouse was small for such bustling city, and the old man imagined they'd need to build something bigger within a few years, especially with the railroad running through. It only stood one story high and could contain maybe ten prisoners at most. The small size was an advantage to the old man.

The walls of his cell were made from field stone and had iron bars set within them. The bars were so tightly spaced that a grown man could not even reach a hand through, never mind squeeze out. The same went for the caged front of the cell.

The chances of escape were slim. He had no weapons but his fists and a bloated leech. Time would not allow him to try and dig his way out, and the limitations of his body stopped him from tearing the iron bars free.

In this case, his size and presence would be a disadvantage. Lawmen didn't take chances with big bastards like him. They kept their distance and cocked their guns. As right they should.

So was this how it would all end? Kicking and pissing over the gallows while a bunch of soft-bellied yanks hooted and hollered? Killed by man's law just a stone's throw away from his showdown with a god? Fading into the blackness of death, just miles and hours away from saving his son?

It was in the midst of these thoughts that the old man heard the scraping of steel against stone coming from behind him. He shot his head around, looking toward the barred window, and couldn't believe what he was seeing. A small pistol was creeping between the bars and scraping against the stone.

At first he thought it was moving of its own volition. A second later, it occurred to him that maybe it was some vigilante who wouldn't wait for the execution and planned to kill him in his cell.

Then he recognized the gun. It was his own backup piece that he had slipped into Hank's pack.

The old man approached the window, and sure enough he saw the boy whom he'd traveled with for so many months now. Hank's small hands were pushing the pistol through the bars.

The old man smiled, and leaned against the window, pretending to stare out at freedom. He mouthed the words "thank you" to Hank. Hank didn't reply, but he pushed the gun all the way through the bars and into the old man's hand.

Once the old man had the pistol secure in his hand, Hank vanished from view. Whether he was afraid of being caught aiding an escape, or he was simply too hurt at being ditched, the old man couldn't be sure. Either way, he was thankful.

The pistol felt good in his hand. It wasn't Donner, but it was iron. Iron would give him the chance to see this whole mess finished. If he played his cards right, he could make it to Winter's End within a few days yet.

The sheriff had taken the old man's coat. Neither his shirt nor his pants would do much for hiding the gun, so he continued to lean against the window. He kept his hands up by the bars, but out of sight from the law. For some time he waited like this, trying to goad out a comment about the loss of his freedom. Eventually he heard footfalls, two pairs, and the jingle of keys.

"Beautiful day out there, huh? You'll be heading for a real nice stroll in a bit. Don't you worry, none," the lawman commented.

The old man responded with a question of his own. "Your pal there that I dealt out some free dentistry too, he like the way that dead rat above your lip tickled his balls?"

"Oh ho ho," the sheriff laughed in a mix of anger and amusement. "No reason not to run your mouth? Think shit can't get any worse?"

The old man continued to look out the window, but answered the man behind him. "Suppose it could. You could try to shove your little prick up my ass. Bet you'd love that, ya dandy."

"Keep your muzzle on him, Bill. I'm gonna teach this old bastard some respect."

The sound of iron against leather verified that the second figure had now pulled his gun, getting ready to cover his partner.

The lawman kept talking, affirming his masculinity and vowing to prove it with his fists. The words were just white noise to the old man. He just kept his gaze out the window, and counted the footfalls behind him.

Once the sheriff had taken enough steps and his voice seemed close enough, the old man whipped around, catching his shorter adversary off guard. A downward elbow to the collarbone dropped the lawman. Almost simultaneously, he fired off two rounds at the deputy with his other hand. Before the subordinate lawman had time to register what had happened the slugs were already blowing out his back.

The sheriff fell to the ground, cursing in pain. A gurgling issued forth from the deputy as he too hit the floor.

In days past, the old man would have pistol-whipped the wounded sheriff and knocked him out. He would have shackled him and gagged him and allowed the man to live another day. Today was different.

Watching the life flee from the deputy, and seeing the pain in the sheriff's face, the old man felt a fearsome hatred overwhelm his mind. It was a loathing so deep and absolute that it rivaled his hate for Thurs.

This feeling was different though. His hatred for Thurs was a steam engine driving him forward. The emotion that consumed the old man now was a wild fire that threatened to overtake his entirety.

Tears of pain reluctantly escaped the sheriff's eyes, as he crawled backwards across the ground. His collarbone had fallen like London Bridge. The broken, pained creature infuriated the old man. Yes, he hated the lawman for the time he had cost him, but it was his weakness that now invoked the old man's unholy rage. The way he crawled and cried like a wounded animal made the old, Confederate warrior thirst for his blood.

On top of all that, the old man now saw that the sheriff was carrying *Donner* in his gun belt. Another thing he loved had been stolen from him, just like his son, his wife, and his nation.

Without thought, at least as man conceives it, the old man cocked the hammer of his pistol and aimed the muzzle toward the pathetic, weak, thieving thing before him.

The black veins in his arm pulsed, like the hearts of vile, independent creatures beneath his skin.

***

A gunshot rang out from the jailhouse. If Hank had been a bit older he might have feared that the law had been quicker on the draw than the old man. This was not the case. The boy had superstitious confidence in the old man's ability. His own father had been a good, strong man. In the end he hadn't had what it took to save the day though.

The old man, on the other hand, had made a life of killing monsters. He had left a trail of dead witches in his quest to put a bullet in the face of a god. Nothing of earth, nor heaven, nor hell could stop the grim, grizzled bastard.

Confident that the old man was doing the shooting instead of being shot, Hank focused on trying to calm down the mottled horse that he had tied to a post across from the jailhouse. The gunshots had scared her, and she was panicked. Hank feared she might kick at him in her desire to break free, so he kept his distance while talking at her in a soothing voice.

"Don't you worry about that banging, girl. That's just my friend coming."

Another shot rang out from inside the jailhouse, and this time the horse stood up on her hind legs, tugging at the rope that tethered her.

"Shush, girlie. No reason to get upset."

People were starting to come out of nearby buildings, eyes toward the source of the resounding gunshots. The attentive crowd was making Hank nervous. It was his hope that he and the old man could sneak out of town without much notice.

He understood why the old man tried to leave him behind. This was the endgame, the final showdown between the man in gray (the old man wasn't quite *man in white* kind of material), and the demon in black. The old man couldn't risk some kid, a Negro kid at that, getting in the way and messing things up. He had his own son to take care of. But now Hank was sure that he would take him along.

Having masterminded a jailbreak, supplying the gun and the horse, Hank knew his worth would be proven to the old man. He'd see that Hank wasn't a kid he had to watch over, but a partner who could cover him as well.

A few minutes passed, and the crowd outside of the jailhouse got bigger. A few men were resting hands on their guns, getting ready to mete out some vigilante justice if it turned out that the law was on the wrong end of those gunshots. Hank's heart began to race and sweat dripped from his brow. Hank was thankful that no one noticed the brown-skinned boy trying to calm the stolen horse.

Finally the double doors to the jailhouse swung open. The old man stood in the entryway, a pistol in each hand, with his sword and pack slung across his back. His artillery coat billowed like the gray wings of some terrible angel. The image was frightening to the folks of Omaha. To Hank it was awe inspiring.

The boy's former master had read *Paradise Lost* to his slaves on more than one occasion. To Hank the old man looked like a modern-day version of Milton's rebel angel, ready to war against the tyrant of heaven. Thinking of the wooden Christ-thing that counseled his father's killer, Hank too was ready for war.

The dramatic revelry of the old man's entrance vanished as one of the men in the crowd tried to draw iron. Without any sign of hesitation, the old man put a .44 slug through the man's face. Less than a second later the old man's smaller pistol found its mark on some poor bastard whose hand was hovering to close to his piece.

There was a distant look in the old man's eyes as he committed these men to dust. He wasn't looking at them, but through them. It was eerie, even to Hank. The boy chalked it up to him being so close to his goal.

The crowd scattered in the wake of the two deaths. The old man stood in the middle of the dirt road in downtown Omaha, looking like someone who'd woken up in the wrong place and wrong time. His eyes scanned the now empty street, trying to make sense of what he was seeing. Finally his gaze came to rest on Hank.

"Come on!" Hank screamed. "We need to hit the road!"

The old man tilted his head to one side, giving Hank a peculiar stare. After a few seconds recollection seemed to kick in, and the old man lowered and shook his head.

"You all right?" Hank asked, more annoyed than genuinely concerned. Of course the old man was all right.

"Yeah. Just a little out of sorts."

The old man didn't run, but he walked swiftly over toward Hank, who was untying the gray mare.

"You steal this horse?"

"I sure as hell didn't buy it."

The old man stroked the animal's neck and whispered an assurance that everything was just fine. To Hank's surprise, the horse began to calm down.

"How'd you do that?"

"Learned a thing or two about calming horses in the war."

The old man placed his foot in the stirrup and hoisted himself into the saddle. He looked down at Hank, who was beaming with pride at having facilitated the escape.

"Anybody see you steal the horse?"

"I think they might have."

"You know they hang horse thieves, right?"

"Then I reckon its better I come with you. At least that way I can die a hero, right?"

The old man rubbed his eyes, seeming to deliberate Hank's sentiment in his mind. After a few seconds he reached down for the boy's hand and lifted him onto the horse's back.

"When you see what's in Winter's End, you might just pray for a chance to dance on the gallows."

Without another word, the old man dug his heels into the horse's side. They sped out of Omaha before any more trouble could show its face.

CHAPTER EIGHTEEN

Emmett had not noticed the door open, or the click of Patrick Silver's boot heels on the floor of his home. It was only when the sheriff had called out his mother's name that he became aware that the bastard lawman had come inside.

"Kylie?" he'd called out.

Emmett wailed his sorrow for a moment longer. His back was to the door and he was kneeling on the floor beneath where his mother hung from a noose that she'd tied to one of the rafters. Her feet still kicked and she choked against the crushing rope around her neck, despite the fact that she'd been there for hours. It hurt him to see her in such pain, rough braids of rope cutting into the skin of her neck and crushing her trachea, but she needed to learn this lesson hard. He had literally gone through hell to save her from death. Such a gift could not so easily be relinquished, and it was disrespect of the highest regard to try and cast it aside. Death would give her a wide berth, and it would take more than a rope and the kick of a chair to convince it otherwise.

He was angry with her. Angry that she would want to hurt him. Angry that she would belittle all of his sacrifices. Angry that she did not appreciate the man he had become.

Most of all he was hurt. Emmett loved his mother more than anything and it broke his heart that she would try to leave him alone in this heartless world.

His feelings toward Silver, however, were not at all mixed.

"You did this!" Emmett's voice was not completely his own. A gravelly, creaking undertone had infected it. If he'd been more in his right mind, he might have recognized it as that other voice in his head.

Silver responded by cocking the hammer of his pistol, but was otherwise silent. Emmett stood up and turned to face the intruder. Silver's head darted from side to side and Emmett realized the man was blinded by the darkness. His weak, mortal eyes had not grown accustomed to the endless darkness of the wastes between the stars. Some small voice inside Emmett questioned why he was able to see in this utter darkness, but that whisper was ignored.

As much as his enemy's blindness was advantageous, Emmett wanted Silver to see. He wanted him to see and he wanted him to fear.

Emmett closed his eyes and raised his hands in front of his face. With his index finger and thumb, Emmett made a shape like a sideways "V". With his other hand, he made an inverse of the same shape, placing his right index finger below his left, and similarly so with his thumbs. A moment later fire erupted from the stove and two oil lamps in the kitchen exploded with fire. The glass shades of the lamps shattered from the sudden, intense heat, and glass showered the room.

Silver retreated several steps back and ducked down as sound and light invaded the room. A sliver of broken glass cut into his left forearm, leaving a deep cut.

The sheriff staggered backward, letting out a shocked cry. He blinked his eyes several times, presumably adjusting to the unmerciful light.

"Look at what you did!" Emmett growled, pointing toward his mother's makeshift gallows.

Kylie Wongraven's still-living body swung gently back and forth from a noose. Deep lacerations adorned her neck, where she had desperately clawed at the rope for God knows how long.

Her fingernails were ragged and broken, covered in the same dried blood that dripped from her neck to her chest. Her body still twitched and her feet kicked in a spastic, un-syncopated manner, which sent droplets of piss from her legs down to the puddle underneath her. Despite her movements, she had given up on escaping the noose, and her arms hung limply at her side.

Emmett stood in front of her. In the firelight, he looked like a nightmare version of his father. His face showed the same chiseled features, but cracked and broken, like some heroic statue that had turned ominous over time. Deep cracks and fissures riddled his dried flesh. Blue eyes, lined with tiny black veins, cried viscous, ebony tears.

"You should have minded your business," Emmett said. "What comes next will not be pleasant."

The thick fingers of Emmett's hands curled with sinister purpose. Blood, piss, and chalk responded to Emmett's semantic gesture, and the circle, which had been left unfinished, closed itself up behind Silver.

"You hurt my mother. You hurt me."

Emmett took a slow step toward Silver and tightened his enormous hands into fists.

"I could make this painless and reap the same gains. A slug to the head. A quick blade across your throat," Emmett growled. "But I want to tear you apart with my bare hands for the sorrow you've brought to my house."

Emmett took another step forward and Silver retreated. Horror and encroaching madness danced in the sheriff's eyes.

"I ain't talking figuratively here, Silver. I'm going to break your bones, tear your flesh, and rend your limbs from your body."

A deep-seated rationality, some part of Emmett that cared more for self-preservation than for vengeance, told him to stop talking and end the man swiftly. The more powerful part of him, that deep voice that spoke to his anger and pain, told him to punish the sheriff and revel in his fear before dining on his pain.

Emmett took another unhurried step forward. He smiled at his prey. Then something odd happened. The fear and threat of insanity fled from Silver's eyes. A grim determination took the place of hopelessness. Not even a second later the lawman had his pistol chambered at his hip. He pulled the trigger and released an explosion of burning lead into Emmett's belly.

To Emmett's surprise, the slug tore through his abdomen, shredding his stomach muscles and his intestines. He looked down at the bloody hole in his stomach and the black sludge that leaked out from it, unsure exactly what had happened. A moment later, the pain, pain more intense than he had ever felt, followed the disbelief.

"I was so close," Emmett muttered as he fell backwards, slamming into his mother's pendulous form on the way down. "So close to heaven and all its power."

The world began to darken. Emmett wasn't sure if the alien force that aided his vision was fading or if he was dying, but he suspected the latter.

His sight had faded, but he could still hear his mother's choked gurgles and a labored breathing that might have been his own, or just as easily Silver's. The hot California air was fading and giving way to the icy grip of hell.

Another explosion filled Emmett's ears and more lead filled his gut. Silver wasn't taking any chances.

The pain caused Emmett to retch, which in turn tore at his already shredded insides, and renewed the cycle of pain induced more retching.

"This can still be salvaged. The door can still be opened!" the growling hateful voice that shared his mind screamed, not in anger but in desperation.

"How?" Emmett asked aloud, in his own voice, leaving his would-be killer to think him delirious.

"The way between worlds can only be opened from the side on which you lie dying. Give yourself to me. Speak the words I say, and give yourself over freely. Only then will the gate open."

Emmett realized now that he would never see those spheres of reality that lay beyond death's realm. It was he who was capable of opening the doorway to infinity, but it was Thurs who would step through. This had been the plan from the start, just as his hateful grandfather and the dark titan had planned.

It was clear now that Thurs was his enemy, just like Poohwi. The pain in his stomach burned like fire though, and the choking sounds of his hanging mother fueled the poison in his mind and blood. Rationality retreated and hatred became his master. His anger should have been directed at the thing called Thurs, or the mad shaman who sired his mother. If he'd been square with himself, he'd have really directed his anger inward.

His rage was becoming a relentless torrent, and it smashed through any logic that might have given it proper direction. At this moment, Emmett wanted the world to burn, and knew himself to be incapable such a task. Instead, he gave himself over to the alien thing inside his mind, and spoke the words of invocation.

***

Wholly unnatural events played out before Patrick Silver's eyes. Fire that had erupted from thin air and bathed the room in an uneven, wavering light. Emmett, his friend's son, lay bleeding on the Wongraven's kitchen floor. Swinging above the boy was the kicking, choking, body of his mother who seemingly refused to die despite the noose around her neck.

Like mother, like son. Emmett kept mumbling incoherently instead of letting the two slugs in his belly escort him into oblivion. The blood pouring out from the boy's gut seemed black in the firelight, as did the bursting veins in his eyes that were now spilling their darkness across the whites and into his pupils.

Beyond reason and belief, Emmett shook off the two belly wounds and pushed himself back onto his feet. A sound like gravel crunching under hooves came from the boy's mouth as he rose. Silver felt as if he were living out a nightmare, and could think of no way out of it but to keep shooting.

He cocked his hammer and took a step away from the monstrous thing before him. As the stomach wounds had not kept the massive creature before him down, Silver chose to aim for the head this time. His hand shook wildly, like an old man with tremors.

The creature, who had once been Emmett Wongraven, staggered forward. Silver thought its slow, awkward shamble was because of the pain of the slugs in him. In truth, the ancient intelligence, which some referred to as Thurs, was learning to control its new body.

Despite Thurs's incredible power, Silver could have thwarted the Devourer's plans right then and there. If he'd not taken the time to steady his hand, if he hadn't waited for an absolutely clear kill shot, then Thurs's earthly form would have been shattered and the evil thing cast back across the abyss.

Patrick Silver waited for the perfect shot, but it never came. Instead, an ounce of lead tore through the back of his skull and exploded out through the front of his face, painting the already grim scene with blood, brain, and bone.

The sheriff's body crashed to the ground. His ruined skull lay at the Titan's feet. Beyond where Silver stood, in the threshold between the sane world outside and the nightmare of the Wongraven house, stood a tall and broad man dressed in Confederate gray. He held a smoking .44 pistol in one hand.

CHAPTER NINETEEN

Winter's End was a fitting name. For the old man, it was where his war would reach its climax and, with any luck, it was the place where he would save his son. For Thurs it was the beginning of a new world, far removed from the cold vacuum of space.

The old man thought back to the day when this all started, for him at least. It had been a bright, beautiful day, and he'd had it in his mind that the sun was mocking him with its eternal optimism. He placed the last shovel full of dirt onto the grave outside of the burnt and broken husk that used to be his home. He looked out upon the ruins of the town that, until only hours before, had been called Affirmation.

That was before the monster inside his son had called upon the earth itself to heave and twist and tear the town to bits. Now it was a graveyard, and the old man was not alone in his loss. There were other survivors, and they too were burying their dead.

The old man had cried, openly and unabashedly on that day, as he patted down the dirt. He was unable to free his mind of the image of his wife's bloody, twisted neck in those moments before he realized that she was ruined. The ragged whisper that crawled its way out from her mouth still echoed in his mind like a Howitzer's report.

His heart ached as he relived telling her that things would be alright, only to have her reach for his gun and silently ask him to put an end to her pain. Sobs and drool and tears escaped him as he heard the report of his pistol echo endlessly in his ears. The image of her splattered skull was burned into his mind forever more.

The thing called Thurs held his son captive, and the old man had known no way to stop it, so he hadn't. It burned like lye on his soul, but he let the thing that had hijacked his boy walk away. He knew it was hurt, and he knew it was afraid, but what could he do? A well-placed shot might exorcise whatever manner of thing had come to possess Emmett, but the old man guessed that it would just as likely end his son's life. He'd never believed in ghosts or gods or monsters and he knew not how to fight them. He would learn though.

Before he'd sent his wife to heaven or hell or that nothingness that lay beyond, the old man promised her that he would save their boy. If it took a week or ten years, he would hunt this thing down and save their son's life. If it took a trail of dead bodies that stretched from Affirmation to Boston, he would make this creature relinquish their boy.

He'd done his best to make good on that promise. He tracked down holy men, witches, and scholars. He'd convinced them to share their secrets, sometimes with a pistol to their head. Those who'd seemed touched from something beyond this world he'd killed. Others he'd left with a sense of pity.

The old man recalled myths told to him by his grandfather, a Swedish immigrant to the States. He remembered tales of monsters from the cold depths of some wasteland called Utgard- that which lies outside. The gods before creation in those stories were titanic, vile, mad things. Giants with souls smelted from anger and hatred.

The old man had never been one for religion, but his experience had taught him that god was real. Only it wasn't some force of love and kindness. God was the rage filled creature from the Old Testament, flooding worlds and wielding plagues. God was a monster, hungry for escape from the frigid depths of Utgard. God was that thing holding his boy captive.

It was just past dawn when Hank and the old man walked into town. They had left their horse a mile or so back, hoping to spare at least her life if things went south. From the looks of things, that was a very likely scenario.

The old man had warned Hank that Winter's End was a witch's den. Anyone who stood between them and the adobe church—that temple of chaos that came together at impossible angles—was to be treated as a monster. The old man had suspected that the whole town might be touched by the Devourers.

They had circled a wide berth around the town and were coming in from the northwest. If Thurs had set up any patrols, they'd be looking for an enemy to come in from the east. At least the old man hoped so.

It seemed he was right. The two companions made it nearly to the center of town before seeing a single soul. Regardless, Hank's hands never left the hilts of his new guns—guns that formerly belonged to the lawmen of Omaha.

At the heart of Winter's End, waiting by the train depot, a hundred or so townsfolk were amassed. The spiritually diseased people of Winter's end were armed with whatever weapons they had found. Some wielded scythes or hammers. Others had more proper weapons like rifles and hunting knives. All, it seemed, were waiting for the train to arrive and for some invader to step off of it.

Hank and the old man took cover behind a barber shop and scoped out the lay of the land. The cultists were fixated on the train depot, waiting for some holy event, such as the ritual murder of Confederate soldier and a former slave, to take place.

The church, which Hank still couldn't look at for more than a few seconds at a time without feeling dizzy, was less than a sprint away. Better yet, they had a clear shot it. All they had to do was stay quiet. That was when Hank saw the look of madness in the old man's eyes.

***

This was it. Thurs waited for him, almost in shooting distance, within the confines of the thing that posed as a church. The mad witches of Winter's End were gathered by the train depot, their backs turned toward the enemy for whom they waited. Sneaking by them would be child's play, and he could then conserve his energy and ammo for the alien god who'd taken his boy.

That was what the rational part of the old man—the human part—said. There was another voice within him that spoke louder. This was a primal, rage-filled aspect, accentuated by the poison in his blood. It was the part of him that was weak to the magic of those what lay beyond. It was that easily manipulated, animal aspect of him that blotted out all reason as he pulled his guns and opened fire on the witches crowded by the railroad tracks.

A boy stood near him, a friend maybe, screaming something. The words were lost beneath the sound of gunfire. It was unimportant, whatever the boy was saying. All that mattered was tearing the life from these vile things before him.

The old man fired both pistols until the explosions turned into clicks. A moment later something jabbed him hard in the ribs. His head whipped around to see the brown child pushing the muzzle of a pistol into his side.

What he saw when looking at Hank was not the boy he'd come to care about. No, what the old man saw was a little nigger pup, the kind that had sunk the Confederacy, threatening him with a deadly weapon.

"What the fuck are you doing?" the boy gasped. The words sounded alien to the old man, and he couldn't quite pick out their meaning.

With his attention fully on the pest beside him, the old man dropped his .44 to the earth, and reached back for his sword.

"You need to wake up! That shit in your blood is making you crazy!" The brown-skinned animal was nearly in tears as it spoke its gibberish.

His massive blade unsheathed, the old man raised his arm for a blow that would cut the child-thing in half.

"Your son is right there!" it pointed at the church, screaming. "Emmett needs you"

Emmett. His son. That was right. He was here to save his son.

The tidal wave of rage and hatred receded from the old man's mind. Reason began to take back hold of him. He shook his head back and forth, trying to exorcise the touch of the Devourers from his soul.

Hank grabbed his hand and tugged him forward.

"We need to run, now!"

The old man looked back to see a mass of witches stampeding toward them. Each wore madness on their face. It was a madness that he had become intimately familiar with. They waved their weapons and shouted curses and evoked the name of Thurs himself. A few fired rifles with wild fervor, but the shots either hit other witches or buried themselves into nearby buildings.

No longer was he compelled by the maddening poison in his veins to waste his time or ammunition on the witches of Winter's End. Now thinking lucidly, he hightailed it to the doors of the church, grabbing Hank up in his arms along the way. The old man was fast, despite his age and the abuse his body had taken. His stride was enormous, given his unusual height, and the boy's added weight was almost imperceptible to him. He easily outpaced the witches.

Unceremoniously, the old man barreled through the doors of god's house—doors that appeared both concave and convex all at once. They were not locked and swung open freely, revealing a massive temple, far larger than it had any right to be, given the confines of the exterior space.

Directly in front of the door lay a walkway of dull granite, riddled with blue veins of lapis lazuli. The walkway stretched out above a churning ocean that existed only inside the church. Pillars of ice stretched upward from below the water to a seemingly endless height on either side of the walkway. These pillars were without number, spaced unevenly out to the right and left of the doorway. At the walkway's end, which seemed to shift distance between only a hundred yards away and some distance barely visible, was the thing called Thurs.

Even in human skin Thurs was something of a giant—at least as tall and wide as the old man. It was kneeling before a primitive stone altar. The creature wore no clothes and its skin was the color of rust, with deep cracks riddling its body. Coarse raven-black hair, like the bristles of an ill-maintained paintbrush, reached down to the floor.

Just through the door behind them, yet as far away as the stars, was the sound of the lynch mob closing in. The old man took his eyes off of Thurs and slammed the doors shut before the oncoming witches could make their way into the church. On this side of reality, the doors were made of black iron and stretched twice as high as the old man. To ensure that mass of witches stay outside the old man shoved his artillery sword through the steel handles of the doors. With the entrance firmly braced, he could focus on the real enemy.

"Have you come here to pay tribute, Confederate?" Thurs spoke without turning toward his two unwelcome guests.

The old man dropped his pack to the ground and began fishing for ammo. He hadn't planned on emptying his capacity before this showdown, so now he had to take advantage of any time he might find.

"A tribute of lead perhaps," the old man said, now loading Donner with six rounds. "Unless you give up my boy."

Thurs stood up in a manner far too graceful to befit his size or monstrous appearance, like some terrible, mountain cat. The titan then turned to face its aggressors. The blood inside both the old man and Hank ran ice cold as the face of the dark titan looked right at them.

The complexion was off, more like the color of the Nevada desert, and the eyes were orbs of jet, but the face... It was like looking at the old man's reflection in a night time lake. Only now did Hank realize what the old man had meant when he said that Thurs had taken his son.

"Thurs .... Thurs is your son?" Hank asked incredulously.

Thurs looked at the two as if it was trying to remember some detail buried deep within its mind—something covered by time and dust. Finally, a look of slow recognition crossed the titan's face.

"You. You are the progenitor." The voice was not Emmett's. It was a gravelly bellow that seemed to come from some place deeper than even the giant's body would allow.

The old man set his calloused thumb against the hammer of his .44 and pulled it back. He didn't raise the pistol though, not just yet. The click of Donner's hammer locking echoed through the abyssal temple like thunder.

"You think your primitive weapons can harm me?" The low register of Thurs's voice ascended into a high-pitched laughter, like the sound of cicada bugs.

Thurs's laughter died. "I am not one of your witches. I am not some terran beast toying with cosmic power. Riddle this shell with holes if you will. I care not."

"Emmett," the old man's voice was shaky, and his eyes were pooling with tears. "Fight it, boy!"

There were two terrible truths to the old man's quest. The first was that he had no real plan. He'd shot, killed, and coerced his way across half a continent. Now faced with the god that inhabited the body of his son, the old man had no idea what to do.

"It's the spider," Hank drew out the words slowly. These words held within them the second horrible truth of the old man's quest. Both the old man and Thurs were too embroiled with one another to note the boy's statement.

"The thing you call Emmett gave itself to me freely. There is no escape from such a bargain."

The old man lifted his pistol and screamed at the nightmare reflection of himself. Tears of pain and rage ran down his withered face and through the gray stubble on his cheeks.

"Give me my boy!"

"No," Thurs answered simply, and turned his back to the old man. Hank noticed the titan smile slightly as it did so. The evil, crack-fleshed thing was enjoying the old man's sorrow. It was feeding off of it.

Thurs kneeled back down at the stone altar, paying the two intruders no further mind.

The old man's hands, always so calm and steady, now trembled. His breath came out as uneven bursts and gasps.

"Take me then!" The words were almost unintelligible, wrapped within sorrow. "You take me and let my boy go!"

Hank turned toward the old man, horrified by what he was asking of the dark titan.

"Your son ain't there!" Hank screamed, anger and fear welling up in his chest.

Again, the old man and Thurs both ignored Hank's protestations.

"Your power ain't meant to be locked up in flesh, and I know that body is damn near breaking. I'm big and I'm tough as nails. I can hold you for a spell longer than you're gonna get from my son."

Thurs looked down at Emmett's hands, which bore cracks in their flesh all the way down to the bone beneath.

"That ain't even your son's body anymore!" Hank screamed, trying to push the old man, as if it might open his mind. "It's like that fungus spider. Ain't a damn thing of your boy left in there!"

The old man didn't even cast a sideward glance toward Hank. It was as if the boy didn't exist. Thurs was the entire world right then, and the giant was slowly rising to its feet. Its naked husk of a body turned and cast a hate-filled smile at the old man. Both he and Hank held their breaths, not knowing what to anticipate from the monster.

"I accept," said the Devourer that wore Emmett's flesh.

Icy cold air poured forth from the eyes and mouth of Emmett's stolen body. The cold front, the true form of that thing called Thurs, poured out from the son and into the father. A cloud of freezing moisture fell to the earth in its wake, leaving a trail of frost between the two.

Hank stepped back, edging closer and closer to the doors as the horrifying vision of the old man's possession unfolded.

The old man's gray eyes turned cataract white, and the poison blood in his body spread like a drop of ink through a pint of water. Every vein and artery showed black beneath his rawhide skin. Thurs didn't need to romance or fool the old man as he had done with his offspring. This time he could take his host immediately. After only seconds it was complete.

With the transfer complete, the shell of Emmett's body hit the granite walkway of the temple and crumbled like a porcelain doll dropped from a child's hand. Bits of brittle tissue fell into the surrounding sea, flash-freezing as they were swallowed beneath the whitecaps that battered the sides of the granite walkway. Hank had been right. There had been nothing left of the old man's son. This thing was not even a human corpse.

While Emmett's body shattered upon the granite, the old man still maintained some level of consciousness. He watched as his last hope on earth literally crumbled to bits. Mercifully, he no longer cared. Taking in the essence of his godly enemy had driven the last vestiges of sanity from him. His mind was consumed with hate and death. Hate for the Yanks. Hate for the savage Indians. Hate for his wife and her sickness that caused all of this. Hate for himself and his numerous failures.

The negativity and madness made Thurs stronger. The emotions fueled him, and the intimacy of seeing the old man's mind unhinge from the inside was a source of utmost pleasure. His gluttonous moment of victory was short-lived, however.

With a steady hand and an expression of serene detachment, Hank did as the old man had taught him. He pulled the trigger of his gun, sending a lead slug through the base of his only friend's skull.

***

The old man's body fell, and a horrible scream, like the sound of a star collapsing, shook the endless temple to its foundations. Pillars of ice began to fissure and split. The freezing sea churned and roared. This place between dimensions, this church of madness, was crumbling at the seams.

The space above the old man's corpse was like a sculpture carved from frozen breath. A ghostly thing, vaguely human in shape, yet mind-bogglingly alien on some fundamental level, floated above the old man's corpse. It screamed its inarticulate rage directly at Hank this time, leaving the boy's exposed flesh frostbitten and covering his clothing in frost.

The force of the scream took Hank off of his feet and slammed him into the iron doors. The breath fled from his body as he slumped on the floor, and he thought that he may have broken a rib. There would be time to fret about broken bones and frostbite later. For now he had to escape this unnatural place.

The boy willed himself to his feet, just as the old man would have done, and used his fear and all of his strength to pull the artillery sword out from the door handles. The stubborn blade would not move. Shards of granite and ice were raining down around him as he as he continued to tug with all that he had. Finally, the sword came free.

Hank dropped the heavy blade off of the walkway and into the angry ocean. The old man had given him many gifts, but some baggage was too heavy to carry.

Thurs swung an icy, incorporeal limb down at Hank. The boy covered his exposed flesh, using his jacket like a shield. The fabric froze stiff, but managed to save his body from further damage.

The titan howled again and pulled back another one of its ghostly limbs. The ice pillars crumbled further and splashed into the frigid sea.

Before the beast could lash out at him again, Hank pulled the massive iron doors open. The sunlight of the place on Earth called Winter's End poured into whatever horrid dimension resided within the church. Waiting in the bright light of the earthly sun was the army of witches who so enthusiastically served the Devourers. Hank chose to take his chances with them, rather than Thurs.

The boy ran through the doorway and dove between the legs of the foremost witch, a balding man in blue overalls wielding a small sickle. The servants of the dark god scurried after the boy, like a group of inept children trying to catch a field mouse. So focused were they on the task of catching Hank for their alien lord, that not one of them noticed Thurs' phantom tentacle lash out from the door, like a whip formed from winter's breath.

Thurs's ethereal limb struck several of its closest faithful, but missed Hank. Their skin instantly turned black and necrotic, and a glaze of white frost formed across their skin and clothes. The ruined, frozen body of the balding witch whom Hank had just outmaneuvered crashed to the ground and shattered like crystal meeting buckshot. The blade of its sickle, turned brittle from the cold of Utgard, hit the ground and exploded into a thousand pieces of frozen shrapnel. Two shards of the frigid metal dug themselves into the back of Hank's right thigh.

Those who had been shielded by their fallen brethren were unharmed but paralyzed by fear and awe. This display of power and force by their master was as holy to them as it was terrifying. It was a miracle, to them akin to the plagues inflicted upon Egypt.

The creaking sound of the frozen bodies shattering behind him only served to inspire Hank's speed. The boy ran with all the energy that a child could muster.

If he'd turned around he would have witnessed the adobe church, with its bizarre geometry, caving in upon itself. He would have seen a billow of white mist, where the warm air of earth met the frigid winds of someplace beyond the stars.

Hank had no interest in looking upon the horrors behind him though. His eyes were fixed on the outer edge of the cursed town. If he'd know the wretched language of the Devourers, he might have heard Thurs curse and beg for a body—*any* body—so that it wouldn't return to Utgard, but all Hank could hear was the pounding of his own heart.

If he believed in happy endings he might have imagined the old man and his boy were smiling down at him from heaven, thanking him for doing what had to be done, but Hank knew that wasn't the case. In real life the heroes failed and gods were terrible things.

Epilogue

The stars were bright, shining their hatred down toward the earth. For those who believed those fires of the devouring armies to be something benevolent, it must have seemed a beautiful night. For the men gathered in this secret grove, it most definitely seemed magical. Not so much for the boy and his mother.

A bonfire, bright and enormous, a symbol of unity with the baleful stars above, burned in the center of the grove. A bit off to the side, just far enough away from the fire, stood massive apple tree, nearly twenty feet tall. Apples were out of season and the branches were bare, save for the noose slung over one gnarled limb.

A young dark-skinned mother kicked and twitched on the end of the hangman's rope as she dangled ten feet above the ground. Twelve men formed a semicircle around the fire and looked on as the woman performed a gallows dance. A thirteenth, a beast of a man at over six feet tall, held the rope in place. All of them wore white robes with masked hoods.

The woman's son, a boy no more than eight years old, younger than Hank had been when the cannibal murdered his father, was forced to watch. The robed figure in the center of the semicircle held the boy's face, and made him witness his mother's dying moments.

The noose had been tied to offer a slow, strangling death, rather than the mercy of a broken neck. Pain and fear were sources of power for these men. But pain and fear could be easily shut down and replaced by hope. Sometimes all it took was a tiny piece of lead.

The sound of thunder echoed through the grove, though no lightning or rain accompanied it. Some invisible force had severed the hangman's rope, and the young mother fell hard to the ground.

Again the sound of thunder rang through the orchard. This time, one of the witches fell. The white robe quickly took on a darker color as the hole in the man's chest pumped out his life force.

The robed servants of the Devourers drew knives and guns of their own from the voluminous folds of their garments. Their fire had ruined their night vision, and the masked hoods hindered their sight even further.

In addition, their bold religious attire and ritual fire made them easy targets. Hank, unencumbered by superstition or servitude, was quite comfortable staying to the shadows.

Hank took several big steps to the right, changing up his angle to keep the witches guessing. His strides were long, as he'd grown to be quite a tall young man. He wouldn't be surprised if the superstitious bastards mistook his calm tactics for supernatural speed.

He fired another round, this time into at the witch who was holding the boy. The Klansman's head exploded, filling his hood with bits of brain, skull, and blood.

Worship of the dark gods what lay outside had grown in the days since the old man left this world and this war behind. It wasn't just angry natives, or weak-minded hill folk. With this new cult, the legion of Utgard now found allies among police chiefs and captains of industry, farm hands and politicians. It wouldn't be long, Hank reckoned, before Thurs or one of his filthy brethren returned to this world.

But Hank had advantages too. He had the shadows and the anonymity of a second-class citizen. He had experience and will. He had the wisdom and memory of the great warrior who had trained him. He had confidence that man would prevail.

Hank let another slug fly, and spilled the blood of a third witch, like a splash of whiskey for a dead friend.

ABOUT THE AUTHOR

Curtis M. Lawson is a writer of unapologetically weird, dark fiction and comics. His work includes the Amazon best-selling novel, IT'S A BAD, BAD, BAD, BAD WORLD, THE DEVOURED, and MASTEMA.
Curtis is a member of the Horror Writer's Association, and the organizer of the WYRD live horror reading series. He lives in Salem, MA with his wife and their son. When he is not writing, Curtis enjoys tabletop RPGs, underground music, playing guitar, and the ocean.

curtismlawson.com
curtismlawson@hotmail.com

Preview- It's A Bad, Bad, Bad, Bad World

Enjoy this preview of Curtis M. Lawson's Amazon Best Seller, *It's A Bad, Bad, Bad, Bad World.*

While The Antique Man lay suffering in the hospital and the two lovers collectively known as the Picasso Killer terrorized and tortured a murder groupie who went by the handle AbsurdByrd_666, another man with an unusual pseudonym of his own was crouching by an open window, watching a U.S. senator through a sniper's sight. The assassin's Christian name was Jack, but to most he was known only as The Rhodesian.

The job he was working was as simple and clean as they came, completely motivated by financial concerns. Politician A was trying to push a law that interfered with CEO B's bottom line. Usually companies in the U.S. didn't conduct business in this way, but Jack's employer was a new-money kind of guy, and he was used to getting his way. Jack wasn't one hundred percent on the details, nor did he care to be. His sphere of concern was bound by his bank account on one side, and his reputation on the other (with strippers somewhere in the middle). Some mercs tried to fight on the side of the angels when circumstance allowed. Jack didn't believe in angels.

He'd made his sniper's nest in the window of an office building across the street from where the senator would be dining. The spot gave a clear view allowing for a clean, easy shot. The place also had a quick escape route which would allow him egress before a 911 dispatcher would even pick up the call.

"Did you know that GMOs are more addictive than heroin?" a slurred voice from the corner of the office questioned.

"I hear that, china. Those pricks in the food industry have me eating two or three times a day. I just can't stop," Jack responded in a gregarious manner.

Just to keep things tidy, Jack had captured and drugged some far-left blogger named Tyrone Wells. Wells was best known for writing scathing and poorly edited calls to arms against the "American Empire." He also had a record for destruction of property. When the police did eventually find The Rhodesian's set-up, they would also find a strung-out Tyrone Wells, with his well-documented fingerprints all over the sniper rifle.

The time had just about come to pull the trigger. The grey-haired lawmaker had been having dinner with a woman half his age at some haughty Italian place with dim lights and pricey wine. The Rhodesian hadn't wanted to ruin an expensive meal for the other folks inside, so he'd waited for Mr. New York Senator to shuffle off toward his waiting town car. He was still arm in arm with the young girl, and Jack smiled, imagining what her face was going to be like in a minute when her sugar daddy's head exploded.

"What are you doing over there anyway?" Tyrone asked, in a confused, drug-addled tone.

"I'm not doing shit. I'm just like a manifestation of your subconscious. But you, fuck-o, you're about to destroy a piece of the American murder machine. Sound good?"

Tyrone giggled and replied with something that sounded like a yes.

The senator's temple was in the center of Jack's crosshairs. Individual hairs were distinguishable in his scope. This would be a clean shot, he knew. He inhaled deeply, getting ready to squeeze the trigger. Before he could exhale, Taylor Swift's voice filled the office, accompanied by horns and drums.

"WTF," Jack exclaimed in an angry whisper.

He let go of his rifle for a moment and reached into his pocket to silence the call. His face was red with embarrassment. Here he was, a world class gun for hire - a soldier since his parents were gunned down in his childhood - and he couldn't remember to shut off his cell phone before pulling an assassination.

"That's not my ringtone," muttered Tyrone. "What's with the pop shit?"

"It's because you're secretly in love with Miss Swift, just like everyone else in the world." There was anger in The Rhodesian's voice, both at himself for the cellphone thing, and at Wells for insulting Taylor's music.

"Truth," Tyrone replied. Damn straight, thought The Rhodesian.

Jack set his scope on the senator again. He was waiting beside the car as his driver opened the Lincoln's door for him and his date. Jack took another deep breath and the cell phone rang again. He muttered an impolite word but this time kept at the task at hand. He didn't want to lose his shot.

Behind him, Tyrone had given in to the pop-side and was mumbling about staying out too late and going on too many dates.

Jack took one more deep breath, ignoring his ringtone and the drug-slurred singing. The world around him vanished and all that existed was his gun and the senator. He exhaled and pulled the trigger. His scope saw nothing but red for a moment, as the senator made his transformation from man to meat.

Curious, Jack moved his scope to the lady friend. She was the image of the Hollywood scream queen - a young and beautiful creature screeching in wide-eyed terror, drenched in blood, gray mattered splattered across her face and dripping down her cleavage.

"Sweet dreams, Jackie-O."

The Rhodesian stood up, leaving his rifle by the window, and walked over to Tyrone, pulling two objects from his pocket. One was his cell phone, which had stopped ringing. The other was a handcuff key. He reached down, uncuffed Tyrone from a heavy desk, and placed the cuffs in his jacket pocket.

"You did it, T. You're a genuine revolutionary now. Just sit back and bask in the glory for a bit."

Jack didn't need to encourage his patsy to stay put. Wells had enough smack pumping through his system to keep him down for another several hours. There was no way he could beat feet before the cops showed up.

All in all, Jack felt the job went pretty well. The senator was dead, and the cops could easily pin it on Wells, which would make them look good. The lack of a real investigation would benefit himself and his client. And as for Wells, well, he'd get some real street cred. They might even put his face on a t-shirt, as they occasionally did with communist murderers.

It was a win for everyone. Except for the senator and his girly, perhaps.

Jack left the office building and stepped into the back alley, per his exit strategy. He looked at his phone and saw two missed calls from his agent. A moment later it rang again.

Jack slid his thumb across the touchscreen, answering the call.

"Seriously, you better be on fire, Holly," Jack said instead of hello.

He walked as Holly spoke on the other end of the line. She rambled on for a minute straight, overexcited about some job, but Jack couldn't quite understand her quick, stumbling jabber. What she ended with, though, made Jack stop dead in his tracks.

"Wait! He's offering how much?"

Jack began walking again as Holly spoke, remembering that he needed to put some distance between himself and the political assassin, Tyrone Wells.

"Ten million dollars? To track down a couple of knives? Is he out of his mind?"

‘

Curtis M. Lawson

Made in the USA
Lexington, KY
06 July 2018